Blood of the Coven

JP Steward

To my best friend and editor:

I would never have made it this far without you, and I'm not just talking about this book. Thank you for always being here with me through what has been the hardest couple years of my life.

TABLE OF CONTENTS

The Letter

The air is brisk. The wind sweeps through the green underbrush and over the streams. There's a hush below the orange and yellow treetops; the gentle rustle of creatures and the soft bubble of streams are the only sounds. Someone walks towards the edge of one stream; their footfalls are light, disturbing nothing. Worn, brown leather boots step up to the stream, the water greeting them eagerly as it seems to reach towards them. They giggle in response as they crouch down, reaching a fair-skinned hand out to run over the water's surface. Reflected in the water is a young witch, Lauren Muldoon, her fiery red hair falling in waves over her shoulders. There's a line of freckles dancing across her nose, which brightens the soft blue-green tone of her eyes.

"I know, long time no see," she says as the water flutters under her fingertips in response. "I've been busy with the coven, taking more classes as expected, but I got some time, and I brought you something!"

The excitement in her voice is palpable as she sits back on her heels, reaching for an old worn satchel. She rummages around in it for a minute before pulling a jar out, then turns back to the water. The jar is full of crystal-clear water and contains a vibrant purple fish.

"I know my coven doesn't care much for water spirits or any magical creatures, so this poor guy was just sitting in class for us to study," she frowns as she holds the jar and pries open the lid. "I knew as soon as I saw him, he looked familiar, so I had to bring him home. If my teacher ever finds out," she gives a strained laugh as she tips the jar over, letting the water spill into the stream, setting the fish free.

In an instant, ten other vibrant, colorful fish appear, darting towards the new addition. It's a joyous reunion as they swim around each other in a tight circle.

"Guys!" she laughs, rocking back on her heels. "You're going to make yourselves dizzy."

With a shake of her head, she turns back and pulls out a bag. Opening it, she shakes it for a second before pouring the grainy brown contents into the water. The fish take to the surface and begin eating. She gives a heavy sigh and folds her arms over her knees as the long black coat sways and surrounds her petite form. "I have a huge summoning project coming up, so I won't be able to stop by for a while. They always dump so much on my plate. I think everyone in the coven has it out for me," she blows a piece of her hair from her face. "I promise, before the stream freezes, I'll be back."

The fish flap their fins at her, which brings a shy smile to her face. She watches the fish for a while longer before they all dart off and vanish. Once the vibrant colors disappear, she pushes herself up.

Before she can reach down to grab her satchel, a shadow moves off to her left, a twig snaps and shatters the silence. Spinning around, she raises her hands, muttering a quick incantation as she waves them towards the bushes the sound came from.

"Lauren, wait! It's just me!" A man's sharp voice shouts in surprise as vines spring up, reaching to wrap around one of his legs. He lets the vine pull him out, hopping on one foot.

Lauren relaxes at the sight of the dark-haired witch.

"Damien," she waves her hand, the vines uncurl from around his leg and sink into the ground. "What are you doing here?"

He dusts off his jeans and scoffs. "Following you, of course," he turns to her with piercing, crystal blue eyes. "A certain fish vanished from Mr. Lewis's classroom, and I had a hunch. So, I followed it."

With a roll of her eyes, Lauren turns back to pick up her satchel after she places the jar back into it. "Now what, are you going to turn me in?"

Damien smiles. "Nah, I'll just inform Mr. Lewis it was you, and you'll receive another detention."

She shakes her head, turning away without a word.

As she makes her way back to their village, he follows with a sly smirk.

"No comment?" he questions. "Come on, Lauren, at least give me some sort of response."

"Damien," there's an edge to her voice, "as much as I enjoy our love-hate relationship, I'm not in the mood for your teasing today. I've got errands to run for my dad and demonology homework to finish before Mrs. Taylor's ridiculous due date."

He shoves his hands in his pockets, clicking his tongue. "Right, you're in some of those upper, upper-level classes. You're quite an overachiever for your age, haven't even settled on a specialty yet."

"I'm not an overachiever," she looks back at him. "I'm just smarter than you idiots."

He curses as he follows behind her.

The fallen leaves crunch under their boots as they take a deer path, looping through the trees and bushes. Damien makes a few more comments, trying to get a rise out of her, but Lauren dutifully ignores him and keeps her lips sealed. The path transitions from dirt to old cobblestone streets as they step into one of the main squares, where most of the coven's shops stand. The square is quieter than usual; only a handful of witches are around. Lauren prays she can leave without incident.

"Alright, Damien," she crosses her arms and tilts her head. "I have to go into town for some errands."

His nose wrinkles in distaste. "You go to the human town too much."

She rolls her eyes. "Humans aren't as bad as everyone makes them out to be."

"You and your brainless father are the only ones who think so," a shrill voice says.

"There goes leaving without incident," Lauren mutters as she turns, flashing a fake smile at the approaching group of witches. "Sarah, always lovely to see you, sis; I see your minions are in tow."

"Half-sis," Sarah corrects with an icy glare. She then smiles, eyes sparkling as she brushes past Lauren to throw herself at Damien. "Babe, what are you doing with her? Is she the one who broke into Mr. Lewis's office?"

He wraps an arm around her and gives her a kiss. "I was confirming that theory; yes, she is."

The other two witches snicker behind Lauren and whisper something under their breath. She glares at them.

"Shall we take her to our High Priest then?" one witch asks as the other conjures lightning shackles.

"Not today," Lauren steps back, "I still have errands to run and work to finish before class tomorrow. So, thanks, but no."

Sarah's nose wrinkles, but before she can make another scathing remark, Damien cuts in with a forced laugh.

"I'm still telling on you. I'm sure you'll hear from the teachers soon," he says as Lauren steps back.

"That's not new," she rolls her eyes. "I'll see you guys in class tomorrow."

She walks away with that last quip and raises her hands, holding one in front and moving her pointer and middle fingers of her other hand in quick circles. The air sparks and cracks open. She mutters a small incantation, and the crack turns into an open portal. The sound of voices, cars, and shopping carts replaces the quiet of the village as she walks through.

On the other side is the human town of Aberdeen, a quaint small town on the edge of the wilderness and just off the main highway, where she and her father frequent for garden and herb supplies. The portal stands in a small woodland area behind the local grocery store, and once she drops her hands, it closes.

She lets out a relieved sigh and relaxes her shoulders as she makes her way out of the woods and into the store. With a focused mind, she takes the store aisle by aisle and collects all the items on the list her father gave to her. Once she pays for everything, she carries the bags back out to the woods and through a new portal.

The homey smell of her kitchen fills her lungs as the portal closes, leaving her standing alone in the dark. She waves her hand in the general direction of the light switch to flip it up. The lights flicker to life and paint the old kitchen in a yellow glow. It's a small galley space, barely enough room for two people to move around together but a decent amount of counter space to work on.

As she sets all the bags down on the counter, she calls out to her father.

There's a moment of silence before she hears a pop, and her father appears beside her. "Get everything?"

"All but something to drown my sorrows in," she pulls everything out of the bags.

"Long day, so I heard," he looks at her from over his glasses as he smirks.

She freezes.

"Mr. Lewis gave me a visit before I left my class," he says as he puts the groceries away. "Turns out, he lost a creature, and Damien says you took it. So does Sarah, but we know her word when it comes to you needs to be taken with a few dozen grains of salt."

"At least you get my sister," she deflates and leans against the opposite counter by the sink. "I did it for a good cause!"

He hums, pushing up his glasses. Once he's finished, he says, "I understand why you did it, Mr. Lewis treats all magical creatures as something to step on, but you got caught. So, you'll serve the time. Which is detention, tomorrow, after your classes."

She throws her head back. "It was a worthy cause."

"I agree," he ruffles her hair, "I love when you're like this, it reminds me of your mother, and proves I raised you well."

"You did a great job on your own," she smiles, "not every dad can be a single dad."

Laughing, he nods his head and rubs the back of his neck.

"Oh right," her smile drops, "speaking of which, I almost attacked Sarah today. Like, I thought about it, but I didn't physically react."

"What did that idiot do?"

She gives a strained smile. "She didn't do anything to me, but she did call us brainless. Same-old, same-old."

He waves it off. "Don't mind Sarah, she can call me brainless all she wants. We know I'm smarter than this entire coven."

"I'm just glad she left mom out of it this time," she says.

"If she had brought up your mother again," he takes a breath as he pushes his hair back. He breathes out with a strained look, and instead of finishing the sentence, he takes the seed packets from the counter and heads out the backdoor.

Her mother is a sore subject. The fact that she knows nothing about her sudden departure sits heavy in her mind. In her father's vague words, she was a healer and the most brilliant witch he knew, but that didn't explain why she left or how Sarah was born.

She follows him to the backyard where they have a large garden. A brown picket fence walls it off from the forest and flowering bushes surround the inside to guard from wandering wildlife. In the center are rows of planters, some with sprouting plants and others with full grown fruits and herbs, ripe for picking. As her father walks to the few empty bits of soil, he pulls his hair into a messy ponytail while she summons a hairband to put hers in a bun. The wind rustles through the trees as they work to plant the new seeds.

As they work, Lauren broaches the topic of her mother.

"Hey, dad," she starts, "we mentioned mom earlier, and I couldn't help but wonder—once again—what happened."

Without missing a beat, her father says, "I told you before, sweetie. We'll discuss that topic when you're older."

"Yeah, you've said, but I'm almost forty. I think I should be able to know by now. I know I look young, but we both know I'm much more mature than I was twenty years ago."

He stares at her and frowns. "You're still a baby witch. I don't make the rules. No one's going to call you a full-fledged adult witch until you're at least fifty, maybe seventy, but definitely once you reach triple digits."

"You haven't even reached triple digits," she smacks his shoulder.

"My point exactly," he taps her nose, then pushes off the ground, "that's why fifty is the low bar."

"Dad," she whines, following him as he makes his way inside. "Come on, now is a good as time as any. You always say I look like mom, I act like mom, hell I'm positive what I did today was what mom would have done!"

"It is," he walks into the kitchen, turning on the sink with a flick of his finger to wash his hands. "As a healer with a nature specialty, similar to you, she was very protective of the forest creatures in this area, but I still don't think it's time."

Lauren continues to grumble as she waves her hand; a hand towel floats from the far counter to her father. He turns off the sink with another hand motion and takes it.

They stand there as he dries his hands. He sets the towel down and gives her a hard look. "You aren't going to drop this, are you?"

"Nope," she pops the 'p' with a grin.

He wraps an arm around her shoulders. "There is so much of your mother in you," he turns them towards the hallway and walks through to the dull living room.

"I have your freckles, though," she points out as they sit on their old and worn beige couch, "and your wit."

"True," he nods his head, "but you still have all your mother's features. If we were humans in a normal town, I'd have soccer moms giving me dirty looks and asking why the Asian man is taking care of the white baby."

She laughs.

"It would have been nice though, if I'd had a son," a dreamy smile lights up his face, "he could look like me. That way, we'd have a matching set of kids."

"Dad," she elbows his side, "you're straying off the subject again."

He clutches his side and leans away, eyes closing in mock pain. After a second, he peaks one open. "My ploy isn't working, is it?"

She rolls her eyes. "Does it ever?"

"Alright, you've worn me down," he sits back up. "You want to know what happened to your mother?"

She nods her head.

"Well," he thinks for a second, "she was the love of my life, still is. The incident which led to all this happened shortly after you were born. I promise I'll keep the details as brief as I can, nothing too graphic."

She wrinkles her nose. "That's gross."

"Hey, you wanted to know!"

"Spill it already!"

"Okay, okay," he smiles. "It was the middle of fall. I had late classes, and your mom went to visit her parents on the north end of the village with you. When I came home, I was shocked to find her back already. I thought it was strange, but she wanted to spend some time alone together and I, being in love, agreed. We ate a wonderful dinner, drank some wine, and ended up in bed."

Her nose wrinkles again as she recoils, "I repeat, gross."

"I repeat, you wanted to know," he points a finger at her. "Now, listen to this next part because the rest of the coven will give you a different story," he waits for her to nod before continuing. "We were talking about the possibility of another kid, when your mother walked in."

"Wait," she blinks a few times, "how does that work?"

"That's what I asked myself. It turns out, when I looked down to see who I was holding, it was your half-sister's mother, Linda. She was the right-hand witch to High Priest and Priestess Kensington back then. She was my rival in everything, and I always knew she hated me. I was so... shocked and hurt that she had gone that far."

"So that's how Sarah came into the picture, but how could she have used magic that skews your vision?"

"I've researched it," he frowns, "and the only thing I could find is demon magic."

"That's forbidden," she blurts out. "I mean, that's what the coven teaches us, but I know better than most witches that since the Salem event, demon magic and demon deals are taboo."

"I know," he places a hand on her shoulder to calm her down, "and, see, I could never prove it. After that night, your mother said she couldn't handle this coven or me; she needed some time. I chased her all the way to the village entrance, but she shifted into her animal form, and I couldn't keep up," by this point, his eyes are glassy, "she was gone before I could catch her."

"Demon magic," she thinks for a minute. "That would explain the feeling I get from your old room, some sort of demon magic that's lingered there all these years. That would have to have been *really* powerful magic."

"You feel it too? I was told I was crazy," he laughs with a tired breath, "told by everyone in the coven that I was just emotional. That's why I couldn't stay in there anymore; most of her things are still in there. I can't bring myself to throw anything away... someday I can try a tracking spell, but I've got too much to do right now. I'm positive she's out there somewhere, and someday I'm going to find her again."

"Your love is inspirational," she rests her head on his shoulder. He wraps his arm around her, pulling her close as he places a kiss on the head.

~

The next day she sits through the hour-long detention with Mr. Lewis. He gives her a lecture on ranks within the coven and listening to authority. By the end, she's ready to fall face-first into her bed, but those plans are derailed as soon as she walks through the front door to find her father in a frantic state.

"Lauren, you're home, perfect," he stumbles through the living room, a suitcase in one hand and an envelope in the other. "I finally got it!"

"Got what?"

"A letter," he takes a second to catch his breath. "I received a letter from The High Coven. They've made an appointment for me with The High Council."

Hell Fire

The words 'High Coven,' and 'High Council,' take a minute to register, but once they do, Lauren steps forward, "We've had no actual contact with The High Coven in decades. Can I see it?"

Her father holds the envelope behind his back as he sets the suitcase down. "High Coven letters are meant to be between them and the recipient only."

"They didn't teach us much about The High Coven," she walks to the couch and sits.

With a wave of his hand, his belongings float out of his room, down the hallway, and fold into the suitcase. "Well, what they taught me is they work in mysterious ways, always cryptic. They only interfere with a coven if they need to. Otherwise, the coven will never hear from them."

"So why did they contact you? I know you've been asking High Priest Kensington to inform the High Coven you want to speak with them since I was a teen, but why?"

"Your mother," he pulls the letter out and unfolds it. "I feel this coven has some corrupt figures in it, namely High Priest and Priestess Kensington."

That piques her interest. She pulls her satchel onto her lap and wraps her arms around it, leaning forward to try to get a glimpse of the paper. Before she can pick out any words, he folds it up and sticks it back in the envelope.

"So, where's the evidence?"

"I've kept it in my room out of your sight," he snaps his fingers; a coat by the door flies to him and slips on his arms, "I know you have my curiosity."

She smiles. "That's fair. What can you tell me then?"

"I'll be gone for a week," he double-checks everything before he closes the suitcase and places the envelope in his coat pocket. "They sent me a train ticket and a second letter with their location. The second letter states to not open it until I'm on the train."

The second letter lies on the coffee table. Red letters that read 'HIGH COVEN OFFICAL' across the sealed edges shine in the light, and the silver wax seal in the center has the letters' MK' pressed into it. It looks official in all regards.

She tilts her head to see it better, and her gut twists. "Dad, that seems odd, though, right?"

He shrugs. "They probably don't want their location to get out; they even said to come alone."

"Dad," she stresses, "that's out of character for The High Coven. I don't know much about them, but I know that."

He shakes his head and gives her a sharp look. "Honey, I love you, but this is out of your element. All you have to do is trust The High Coven."

Even though she disagrees, she nods her head.

He turns away and walks down the hall. She knows she hasn't spent enough time around darker magic to know it well, but she feels something dark in the letter.

"Do you leave tonight?" she asks as he returns to the room.

"They want to see me ASAP and worry I might be followed if I wait too long," he picks up his suitcase. "The train arrives shortly, so we have to go."

"We?"

"Yes, I want you to come with me."

Before she can protest going with him, he grabs her arm, skin-to-skin, and teleports them.

Teleportation is disorienting for those who don't specialize in it, but being unprepared can throw anyone off balance. When they reach their destination, a small parking lot, Lauren falls to her knees and tries to catch her breath.

"Dad!"

"Sorry," he tries to hold in a laugh, "but we needed to go, now come on."

He helps her stand up and they walk to the train station. As they step onto the platform, she takes a minute to think over her words before speaking up.

"Dad," she says, "I know I don't know much, but you taught me to trust my instinct, and right now, my instinct is telling me that, this," she points to the envelope in his hand, "is not good."

At first, he doesn't respond. He hums in acknowledgment without looking at her.

The silence is stiff. She thinks she may have crossed a line, and he keeps his silence until the train comes in sight of the station.

"I know I told you to trust your instinct, but," he looks at her, pauses, then gives her a sad smile, "I honestly worry that you not having a specialty makes you susceptible to delusion."

She opens her mouth to refute his statement, but he cuts her off.

"High Priest Kensington has talked to me about it. Not having a designated specialty can make you dangerous."

She stands frozen as the train rolls onto the platform.

"For this," he holds up the envelope, "I have to trust my instinct."

She wants to press the matter, ask where this information comes from, but she's too stunned. Even though he didn't slap her, it feels like someone did. All she can do is nod her head and close her mouth in a tight line.

Her father reaches over and pats her head. "I promise I'll be back before you know it. While I'm gone, spend some time thinking about a specialty or two, okay?"

"Okay," her voice is weak; she keeps her eyes downcast.

"Good," he gives her a tight smile and a kiss to her head. "I love you."

"I love you too, dad."

With those parting words, she steps back and bites at her nails as she sits on a bench. She could make a portal to go home, but she doesn't; a voice in her head tells her to stay, so she does.

It takes a few minutes more for the train to board. It slowly begins to move and then picks up speed. The unease builds as she watches; it grows and grows until a flash of light from one of the train cars catches her eye.

Then it explodes.

The windows and doors blow out, and the ground shakes; fire and smoke billow out with a ferocity only matched by hellfire. The shock wave derails the last few cars, they skid into the road, but the main car stays attached as the brakes screech.

Once the train stands still, the fire still crackling into the air, Lauren moves into action.

Sirens sound out in the distance as people climb out of the cars. Passersby help people climb out of the cars and walk to safety. Lauren joins a group as they pull people out of the car next to the burning one. The heat of the fire is almost unbearable; the intensity reminds her of her demonology lessons on the raw energy of hellfire in the physical world.

With every person they pull from the wreckage, she desperately checks each face for her father. Before she can approach the fire, the firefighters arrive, and a police officer grabs her arm.

"You need to step back," he says as he moves her to join everyone else.

"My father might be in there," she looks to where the firefighters are now spraying the flames. "I can't find him—"

Another explosion sends them both to the ground. Thick, black smoke billows into the air and darkens the sky.

Lauren freezes, gaze stuck on the melting metal. Pieces of ash and debris fall from the sky, charred paper and clothing float down around them. One piece of paper falls at her feet. She pays it no mind, but then a ray of sunlight strikes it, and it shines into her eyes. She looks down at her feet and sees a piece of an envelope, the envelope given to her father. She moves to her knees and reaches out for it, noting the charred edges and the silver seal still intact. Her hands shake. The magic on the unmarred seal stings her fingertips as she lifts it up. The uncertainty and worry return, and she understands why.

This magic is powerful. It's dark and painful.

The police officer stands and finds a few of the train's crew. He asks them for information on the passengers as Lauren pulls herself up to her feet.

"There was only one man in that car," one crewman states.

"Was he on the platform with this woman?" The police officer reaches out to take her arm.

The crewman looks her over.

She holds her breath.

Then he nods his head.

"I'm sorry, miss."

The air disappears from her lungs. She clutches the envelope piece in her fist and blinks as she looks around. Tears blur her vision. She opens her mouth, but no words come out, so she snaps her mouth shut and lets out a shaky breath. She shakes her head and squeezes her eyes closed.

"No," she shakes her head again.

She opens her mouth to speak again, but a sob comes out as the tears break free. The police officer reaches for her, but she steps back and covers her mouth as the tears roll down her cheeks. She turns away from the crowd of people and looks at the wreckage, her gut twists.

The fear and the panic take over and she runs. All noise fades to static as she runs down the road; her legs carry her away from the wreckage. She runs to the woodland, into the trees, and away from prying eyes as her emotional distress forces her to shift.

One minute she's on two legs, and the next, she's on four.

There's still water in her eyes as her fox form barrels through the woods like a copper blur. It isn't until she reaches a highway that she skids to a halt. She ducks into the underbrush as her body shakes from head to tail.

It takes a while for her to gain enough control over her magic to shift back to her human form. Once shifted, she stays on the ground, her hands holding onto the ground as she tries to catch her breath.

Dad is dead.

Those words repeat in her mind. She shakes her head to clear it before she sits up on her knees. A sharp pain pulls her from her thoughts. She looks down and sees her torn jeans; open gashes all along them. The pain keeps her present long enough to create a portal home and push herself through.

As soon as she hits the carpet, she breaks into heavy sobs and begins to gasp for air. The scene continues to replay in her mind eye. She crawls back so she can rest against a wall, then she wraps her arms around her knees and cries harder.

It's a while before she can do anything but cry. Her emotions bleed into her magic and the plants in the house begin to wilt.

There's a dull ache in her chest and she has a single thought that pulls more tears from her bloodshot eyes.

"I need to inform the coven."

Kensington

The full moon casts a blue glow over the village. The gentle hue soothes Lauren, but the ache is still present. She takes a second to close her eyes and soak up the moonlight before she makes her way towards the coven's town hall.

The town hall is where all official coven business occurs and where High Priest and Priestess Kensington live. It's the second tallest structure in the village, with black spires that point towards the sky. Lantern light emits a warm glow from inside, and there's a large stone staircase that leads up to the two hearty oak doors. In most situations, witches must use the bronze knockers to announce their presence, but in this dire situation, Lauren lets herself in.

The doors close behind her, and the sound resonates throughout the building. A coven member emerges from a room to her left.

"Muldoon?" The witch says, "what's wrong?"

"I need to see High Priest Kensington," her voice gives away her distress as it wavers.

The witch nods his head and beckons for her to follow. They walk down a hallway and through an office door.

"High Priest Kensington, Lauren Muldoon is here to see you," he ushers her in and gives a brief bow, then leaves.

In front of an ornate desk sits a tall witch. His hair is steel grey, his eyes an icy blue, and his skin is sickly pale. He doesn't look up from the worn, leather-bound book on his desk. Lauren waits for him to address her with her hands clasped together. The High Priest places a bookmark in the book and closes it.

"Lauren," he says, "what brings you here at such a late hour?"

"I have some," she pauses and takes a shaky breath, "uh, news that will affect this coven."

She hesitates to continue. The High Priest waves his hand.

"My father, Suho Kim, has just been killed," she holds back another wave of tears, "he was on his way to see the High Coven, and the train he boarded blew up."

Realization dawns on his face as he leans back. "The letter I delivered to him this afternoon, yes, I remember. And you say he was killed? Don't you mean he died?"

Lauren shakes her head. "No, this whole situation was weird, and I may be emotional right now," she wipes her eyes clear of tears, "but I know this wasn't an accident."

He hums and nods his head. "Well, I'm deeply sorry for your loss. This will not sit well with the coven. You said it was a train explosion?"

As she nods her head, he moves his book aside and grabs a stack of small papers.

"Okay," he takes a pen and writes, "that sounds like a human accident."

"The letter he received was strange, and it didn't feel right. I felt the letter had dark intentions."

He stills his hand and glares at her, "I'm sorry, but it almost sounds like you're accusing the High Coven of murder?"

"Well," she hesitates, "yes, but no. I'm not sure if the letter even came from them."

"I can assure you, the High Coven sent that letter, and they did not blow up a train. I will have to inform them as soon as possible about your father's tragedy," he sighs and jots down a few notes. "As for the cause of death, are you sure it wasn't you who caused the explosion?"

"Um," she tilts her head, "I'm sorry, sir, but how could I have caused it?"

He places the pen down and folds his hands together. "Recent research has shown that when a witch does not pick a specialty by the time their basic schooling finishes, they become more and more volatile and their magic becomes unstable."

Her father's words echo in her head as she curls an arm around her waist and looks away.

"You never even considered picking one from what your teachers say," he turns to the side, reaches down, and pulls out a file. "I was just explaining this to your father earlier this week. You are the only coven member who hasn't picked a specialty."

She tries to comprehend how her simple magic could be volatile. In her heart, she knows that elemental magic–especially fire–is not her expertise. She also knows hellfire isn't something even Damien, an elemental specialist, could conjure.

"Sir, with all due respect, the magic I felt coming from the train was much darker in nature than any magic I can conjure."

"Darker?" He lays the file out in front of him. "Well, you have been extremely interested in demonology these last few years. It could be your specialty shining through."

"Sir," she raises her voice, "I'm trying to be serious; I understand I need to pick a specialty, but there's no way I could conjure pure hellfire."

Silence follows.

Lauren tries to gauge his reaction. Shock appears on his face for a second, then he grins.

"Well, that poses a dangerous issue," he chuckles to himself. "You are on house arrest until we sort this out."

"Wait, what?"

"You heard me," he snaps his fingers, and the door opens, "house arrest. We'll look into the situation tomorrow, but for now, go home and stay there."

Before she can do anything, a pair of witches enter the room and seize her. As she's being escorted out, she hears the High Priestess call out her husband's name followed by his reassurance that nothing is wrong as they sweep her off into the night. They drop her off and then wait for a pair of guards to be appointed to her door before returning to Kensington.

With nowhere else to go, she turns in for the night. The emotions, the stress, and the loss finally catch up with her as she feels sleep overcome her.

As the sun rises the next day, Lauren finds herself in a new world. She's awoken by shouts from outside. She pulls her curtains back to see members of her coven. Though there aren't many, the news of her father's death seems to have spread, and they are there to voice their distaste for her. One of them spots her through the window and starts shouting curses, so she closes the curtains and hides inside. She tries talking to the guards and asks for information on what they've been told, but all they say is that her half-sister is who she should speak to. Their tone puts her on edge, so she retreats once more.

The day drags on until Damien shows up and has the guards let him in. He walks in and sees Lauren in her living room. She pays him no mind even though she heard him enter; her eyes remain fixed on the wax seal she placed on the coffee table.

"So, your sister says you killed your father," he says.

Lauren scoffs and rolls her eyes. "That's what's going on? I was told there would be an investigation."

He walks over and sits next to her. "Supposedly, there was, and they found that your magic is too unstable, and your anger led to you killing your father. Accident or not, they have accused you, and the coven kind of wants to see you hanged."

Chills race down her spine. She lets out a shaky breath. "I bet that was my sister's idea?"

He nods. "If it's any consolation, I don't think you killed him."

She eyes him.

"Seriously," he places a hand over his heart, "honest to the High Coven. According to this fire elemental, I don't think you have it in you."

Her eyes narrow into a glare. "What the fuck does that mean?"

"Don't get defensive," he laughs and pats her head, "it just means that I don't think you have enough hatred in you to produce fire. You strike me as more of a nature and healing specialty witch, but right now, the coven won't hear any arguments for you."

"Great," she draws the word out, and she sinks into the couch. "So, what now, I just sit here and wait to be hanged?"

"I mean," he pauses, looks around, then leans closer and says, "you could run away. I honestly don't think they'd come after you."

She stares at him. "Seriously?"

"Yeah, seriously! You could be one of those witches who starts their own coven. I think it'd be cool."

She thinks it over. It's an appealing idea, but this is her home despite everything. How could she leave?

Not long later, he leaves with one last piece of advice, "I would make your decision fast, though. They plan to have your trial and sentencing by tomorrow."

Once alone again, she turns her attention back to the seal. She can't get her mind off it, and it still buzzes with dark magic. As she stares it down, she feels something familiar; it tugs at the back of her mind and pulls her attention away from the seal, and makes her stand up and look down the hallway at the door to her mother's room. She hesitates, but she picks up the seal and moves towards the room.

With a flick of her wrist, the lock turns, and the door clicks open. As she pushes the door open, the stench of dark magic hits her and buzzes in unison with the seal's magic.

The room looks as if time forgot about it. Dense layers of gray dust coat every surface from the unmade bed against the far wall to the dresser next to the door. There's a stillness to the air that makes her feel as if she opened the door to another time. It would almost be peaceful, if not for the presence of dark magic.

"Of course," she steps into the room. "The same people who got mom to leave would be after dad. That makes sense. Maybe," she wanders to the closet in the corner, which is full of dusty dresses. "Maybe mom would know what to do," she walks over to the dresser. An old jewelry box on top draws her attention, but she looks away. "I could try to track her, but I'd need the right spell and an object with her essence attached to it."

She examines each object around the room before she walks across the hall to her father's room, where she hopes to find something. Her hands shake as she's hit once more with the realization that he's gone. Tears form, but she blinks them away as she opens the door.

Compared to her mother's room, her father's is in pristine condition. Aside from a bed, there's not much in the room except a desk which has different stacks of papers strewn across it. She walks to the desk and pulls out the chair, sitting down as she places the seal in an empty spot. Then she sifts through the mess.

Most of the papers are handwritten notes, others are official documents from the coven, and some are neatly written letters about her mother and events in his life. None of it is organized, so she starts to go through every piece of paper and read it all.

The night wears on, and soon enough, she grows tired. She sets the papers down and rubs her eyes. As she goes to stand up, a letter seal catches her eye. An old, yellowed envelope sits on the back corner. The seal in the center is bronze and similar to the one her father received, but the letters inside the wax seal read 'HC' instead of 'MK.' She grabs it and runs her finger along the red 'HIGH COVEN OFFICAL' letters as she studies the seal.

"Wait a minute," she grabs the seal from the recent letter and places it next to the older seal.

Side by side, the seals look almost identical. She stares at them, and then it clicks.

"High Coven. Kensington," she taps the 'MK,' and thinks for a minute more. "The

High Priestess calls him Michael, so his full name is Michael Kensington."

The pieces fall into place, fitting together as she sifts through the papers once more. She sees that each neatly detailed document about events in their coven is the documentation for a case against her coven to be presented to The High Coven.

"Dad was trying to prove our coven was corrupt," her shoulders drop, and bile rises in her throat, "and they killed him for it."

Witch on the Run

The village is cast in shadows as the sun sinks below the trees. Lauren lights a few lanterns to create enough light to see.

She takes her satchel and makes her way through the house, collecting items from clothes to food, spell books to jars of herbs and seeds, anything she can think will be necessary for her journey. Then she heads to her father's room. As she gathers all his evidence, she fights back an onslaught of despair. The tears form, but she refuses to cry and wipes them away.

To get her emotions in check, she heads to her mother's room to search for something she can use for a tracking spell.

Her mother's belongings are too old to hold traces of magic or memories. Layers upon layers of dust coat every surface and dull out their potential. It's been close to forty years; the magic traces are gone.

She takes her time to walk around and run her hand over each piece. Frustration makes it hard for her to focus.

"Nothing in here has been touched since she left," she sighs; then the jewelry box catches her eye again.

She looks at it for a few seconds, then she walks over and pulls the lid open.

Inside are two items: a black leather necklace with a metal pendant and an old Polaroid photo. The pendant is a triquetra knot with a fox lying inside it; the metal shines and vibrates with old magic. The Polaroid is faded; two figures stand with smiles on their faces as they hold each other. This is the first clear image she has of her mother, and she understands why her father says they look alike. In the picture, her mother is wearing the necklace, and her curiosity peaks, but then she realizes she can't ask her father about it. What is its significance? Did he give it to her? When is the photo from?

A wave of grief crashes over her; she crumples to the floor and uses her hand to hold herself steady as she cries. The wound is still fresh, one wrong thought tears the scab open, and the heartache takes hold of her.

The last rays of sunlight are a hazy hue on the horizon line when she pulls herself together. Her legs shake, but she forces herself to stand, grab the photo and necklace, and leave the room. She places the picture in her satchel and puts on her mother's necklace as she steps into the living room.

A chill runs down her spine and causes her shoulders to curl inward as she looks around. The air shifts; she realizes this will be the last time she sees this house.

Forty years worth of memories flash before her eyes. The thought of leaving never came to her mind, even with how horribly they treat her. This is her home. Tears slide down her face, but she wipes them away, then lifts her arms and opens a portal as she gives one last look. Then she leaves.

The portal takes her to the bank of a river opposite her coven's land. She knows from this spot she can walk to the closest, largest human city. She hopes it's the last place her coven will search for her if they try to come after her.

It takes one day for her to hike across the countryside. She hunts in her fox form and cooks herself a quick meal in the woods before she heads into the city. The sun has set by this point. She digs out some human cash from the bottom of her satchel and buys herself a cheap motel room for the night. Inside and away from her coven, she lets her emotions out, and then the exhaustion takes hold as she cries herself to sleep.

In the morning, she buys a map of North Carolina and sits down at a diner. As she eats breakfast, she takes out a pencil and marks down her coven's landmarks on the map to find a blind spot to sneak through or hide in until she can perform a tracking spell. She takes her mother's pendant between her fingers and twirls it around, finding comfort in the motion.

After a while, she decides to find a town to hide in. A little place where no one would think to look for any human or witch. Somewhere secluded and private enough to perform a tracking spell.

She spends one more night at the motel with the plan set before venturing west into the wilderness unclaimed by any covens. She makes her way up the mountains in search of the perfect town.

On the second day of her journey, she finds the tiny town of Highlands.

The sun rises into the crisp air as she strolls down the sidewalks and takes in the town. She needs to find a place to stay, but motels are too expensive given the meager amount of human money she has left. A house is only an option if she uses magic to trick the owner and gain access. Since she's not sure what to do next, she stops at an intersection. She stands there for a minute, and then an old, green building catches her attention. The sign on it reads, "Sweet Treats Deli," and the thought of food triggers her stomach, so she heads in for a bite to eat.

The inside of the shop is updated, clean, and white with a fresh modern feel. It's small and quaint. She walks past the booths, up to the counter, and orders a couple of items to eat; then she takes the food, sits down, and thinks over her options. Lying isn't unfamiliar to her, and she can make up a story about being a college student on a solo trip in need of a place to stay with no problem. No one would question it. She isn't sure who to ask about rental cabins, though.

The door of the parlor opens, a cool breeze and high-pitched laugher sweep through. Two hispanic men enter hand-in-hand, with matching smiles. The one who laughs has a hand over his mouth; he's the shorter of the two, with a lean frame and vibrant fluffy lavender hair that makes his naturally tan skin seem even darker. His other half, of similar skin tone, has a captivating aura around his broader frame and sharp eyes beneath his dark wavy bangs, but they soften as he smiles down at his partner. They talk in light tones as they walk up to the counter. She hears the cashier greet them with a warm familiarity. She concludes they're locals, and they or the cashier may have advice on where to stay. She finished eating as the couple sits down, then once she's done, she approaches the counter.

"Excuse me, I'm new in town on a college winter adventure," she laughs and put on a pleasant smile, "I want to find a place to stay that's not the usual hotels or motels, and I was wondering if you know of anything in town?"

The cashier hums and leans on the counter. "We have a few folks who rent out renovated cabins, mostly for couples, though. You traveling solo?"

She nods. "Yeah, I wanted to spend some time by myself before I graduated."

"That's cool," he gives her a genuine smile before he looks over her shoulder towards the booths.

"Hey, love birds."

The short one's head perks. "What?"

"This girl," he points at Lauren, "is looking for a non-hotel place to stay. Who's the guy who just renovated all those cabins? I thought he was renting them out."

"He is," the taller speaks up this time, "what was his name? Charles? Christian?"

The other chews on his straw as he tilts his head. "No, wasn't it," he sits back and claps his hand, "Chase! Chase Reilly."

"Right!" The cashier grabs a pen and napkin. "He's supposed to rent them out soon. Here's his contact info."

"Thank you, so much," she makes sure to smile at them all before she takes the napkin and leaves with a promise to see them around town.

As she steps out, she pulls out her phone and calls the number; she speaks to the man, and he agrees to show her a cabin that is ready to rent. He gives her the address and directions, then meets at the cabin and gives her a tour of the small cabin space. There's a single bedroom and bathroom, and the living room and kitchen are combined with access to the front and back, which is an open grassy area that leads off into the forest.

"It's cute," she says as they step back out front, "very secluded."

"There are a few houses nearby, but all these trees," he makes a gesture towards the forest surrounding them, "keep it private."

"I like it; I'll rent it, but first," she rolls up her sleeves and steps forward. She presses her hand against his forehead; blue sparks jump from her fingertips and shock both of them as searing pain shoots up her arm.

"You know you're renting this house out," she begins as the man's eyes glaze over, "but you will not speak about the person, and you won't question why there's no money going into your account. You won't even remember this encounter in the future. There's nothing strange about the girl. She's a college student on vacation. You will get back in your truck and go home," she takes a deep breath and sends another wave of sparks out of her hands as the man stumbles back.

She releases his forehead, and he blinks several times. Still in a daze, he turns to his truck and climbs in and drives away.

It isn't until the sound of the tires fades that she lets herself fall. Her knees slam into the ground as her body shakes.

She tries to catch her breath and mumbles, "I forget how much energy mind control incantations take."

Stepping inside, she dumps her satchel on the couch and digs out an energy potion and downs the crystal blue liquid.

While she waits for her energy to replenish, she sets up her things around the house and a potion brewing station in the middle of the living room. By the time her energy is back, she has everything done, and the need for food arises. She places a glamor over the house as a precaution and heads to the local store.

As she goes up and down the aisles to collect essential food items to keep her stocked for the next month. She stops in the tea section to look through the flavors and brands while judging them based on the ingredients. Then, a honey tea on an upper shelf catches her eye, but it's just out of her reach.

She takes a second to gauge if she can reach it, then she places her foot on the bottom shelf and attempts to grab it.

"Here, let me," a voice says.

A hand reaches over her head; she flinches away and looks back to see a tall Asian man beside her. He grabs the tea and flashes her a bright smile. He's handsome, with silver hair, soft brown eyes, and has a fancy fur-lined coat that hangs off his athletic frame. His style and aura make him stand out against the dreary store aisle.

"Thank you." She says politely.

He tilts his head. "You must be the new girl. College road trip, right?"

"I am." She forces a pleasant smile to play the part, "I guess news spreads fast in a small town."

"It does," he gives a good-natured laugh and holds the tea out to her.

She grabs the box and pauses as their skin touches. His smile widens.

"It's such a small town that most people forget it's even here," there's a bite to his words, a tone that sets her on edge.

She pulls her hand back and turns away to place the tea in the cart. "Well, I won't be here for long. I won't even be out of my cabin much."

With her back to him, she doesn't see the momentary shock on his face as he steps back. Then her shoes slip, and she stumbles. He steadies her with a hand on her wrist as he tries again. "People move on and forget about this town. There are many other mountain towns that people find themselves in instead of this one."

"Well," she pulls away again, "I'm sure I'll forget after I leave, but for now, I'm going to finish shopping. Thank you again."

He hesitates as she walks, but he says, "No problem," and continues to watch her until she turns the corner.

For the rest of her time in the store, she doesn't see him, but a chill tickles her neck.

When she returns to the cabin, she puts the food away before going into the back area to create a makeshift garden for the tracking spell ingredients. She conjures a heat shield to protect the plants as she pulls out the seeds and potions of growth; by sunrise, they'll be almost full grown. Once she finished, she heads inside and goes to bed.

In the morning, she wakes with a pleasant lightness to her body. The emotional fatigue still lingers, but she feels refreshed. She starts the day by reading over her spell books, studying the different tracking potions and spells while taking notes. It doesn't take long for her to lose track of time, and it isn't until there's a knock on her door that she snaps out of her focus. She looks at the clock on her phone to see it is after noon as another knock comes from the door.

She places the book down and walks to open the door where she meets a friendly faced man of obvious Asian descent. He has soft features, black hair that sweeps down his forehead, and he's dressed in a sweater and jeans, which accent his height.

"Hi," he greets as he holds out his hand, "I'm Minseok; I live in a cabin nearby. I heard Chase rented this cabin out, so I wanted to give you a warm welcome to Highlands."

"Thank you, it's nice to meet you," she shakes his hand. "My name's Lauren."

He lifts his other hand to reveal a basket. "I baked some muffins and pastries for my roommates, and I had some extra; I thought it would make a great welcome present."

A warmth fills her chest as she smiles, genuine and soft, as she takes the basket he offers. "You didn't have to. This is too sweet!"

"We don't get a lot of new people who stay here, so I thought," he shrugs, "why not."

"Thank you, seriously."

"You're welcome. I hope you enjoy it here," he gives her a wave with both hands and flashes a full toothy smile before he heads off.

The warmth doesn't leave her for the rest of the day.

She eats a couple of the muffins with lunch; she savors the sweet treat as her mind wanders to her father and the times they used to bake together. This train of thought brings tears to the equation, which she forces down.

Once she finishes her food, she heads to the makeshift garden to tend to the plants and fight back the depressive thoughts of her father. She manages to stay strong for a while, but finally the emotions win, and she breaks into heavy sobs as tears pool in her eyes.

A snowy owl appears from the sky. It dives and settles on the edge of the roof. It looks around before its yellow eyes find her, and then it chirps at her.

"Hey friend," she sniffles as she wipes her eyes, "a little early for you. It's not quite snowing yet."

The owl swoops towards her and lands on the ground beside the plants. It sticks its beak out towards the plants.

"Hey!" She reaches out a hand and the owl to hoops back. "Don't mess with these. They're important. I need these for a tracking spell."

The owl spins its head sideways and stares at her.

She gives it a closed-lip smile and rests her hands in her lap. "I'm sure you aren't here to hear a poor witch's sob story about horrible covens and family tragedies. I won't bore you, I promise."

The owl chirps and hops closer to her.

"I don't have any lemmings or mice for you, but I have these," she leans over and plucks a few leaves off one plant. "These are energizing herbs."

She sets the herbs down in front of the owl and waits.

At first, it eyes the food, then leans down and slowly nibbles on them.

She relaxes and sits down. "I may not be an animal specialty, but I think being a nature specialty is still pretty close. Nature and something else. I'm still not sure yet."

The odd pair sits in comfortable silence. Occasionally, she talks about little things from her travel or facts she knows about herbs and plants. The owl eats and sits, chirping every once in a while as she continues to work with the plants. The sun has fallen behind the horizon by the time the owl shakes out its wings and takes flight.

"You're welcome," she says with a smile. "I still have a way with animal's that's for sure."

She watches as it disappears into the trees, blending into the dark forest. There's a thin veil of light that hugs the treetops, so she calls it a night to get enough sleep before she begins the true task of creating and testing the tracking spell.

The Local Coven

The day Lauren arrives, the local coven leader feels an enormous burst of magic come from town. His blood boils because the two trouble makers of his coven are the only ones in town, and he isn't aware of the new witch. He makes his way back to their home, a simple yellow house just off the main road and up a steep driveway; a glamour keeps it hidden from any human car or jogger that may pass by. He storms up their driveway and slams open the front door. He rips off his scarf and throws it on the dresser by the door while roughly kicking off his boots as he runs a hand through his silver hair.

A witch in the kitchen, which can be seen from the entryway, makes a noise of protest and glares at the boots and freshly scuffed wall.

"Hongjoong, is there a reason you're storming in like a child?" he asks while he sets down a plant he had been trimming.

Directly across from the open kitchen, hidden from Hongjoong's view, is their living room where a single black couch and coffee table fill most the space. The back of the couch faces the kitchen, and a dirty blonde head of curly hair pops up over the back to watch the interaction.

"Minseok, where the hell are the huskies?" he asks with a sharp tone as he stomps into the open space between the living room, dining area, and kitchen and scans the open area.

"Tamryn said they left already," Minseok says, to which Tamryn, the witch on the couch, gives a hum of affirmation. "What's the big deal? And did you get my ingredients?"

Hongjoong pulls his backpack off. "I did. Our heavy snow is coming, though, so this may be the last batch." He sets the pack on the kitchen counter. "As for the big deal, there was an enormous amount of magic used in town, a burst of a dark magic."

"Well, I'm sure they have a reason, and they'll tell us when they get back," he notes the shake in Tamryn's hand that rests on the back of the couch and sighs. He takes Hongjoong by the shoulders and pushes him to the couch as Tamryn, who's a rather scrawny witch, sits up properly. "Now, calm down. I am going to make some tea. And you are going to apologize because you scared the baby."

"I'm not the baby," Tamryn turns his gaze to the book in his hands as he shuffles into the corner of the couch, making his already small frame take up less space.

Hongjoong sits in the free space, while Minseok returns to the kitchen and grabs the kettle, keeping his watchful eye on them.

"I'm sorry," Hongjoong rubs his face and rests his elbows on his knees.

Tamryn shrugs, eyes fixed on the book. "You don't often shout anymore, so I'm good. I'm also not the baby; Hatawa's the baby."

"By age, he's the baby, but by circumstance," he smiles, "you are the baby."

As his face grows warm, Tamryn shuffles and says. "The lovebirds headed out a while ago. I'm sure they'll be back soon. Joshua went for a run, the rabbit is sleeping, and Hatawa is doing something, but I don't know what; I honestly wasn't listening."

Minseok snorts.

"Things never change."

Aside from the snip of plant shears and the flip of book pages, the house is quiet. Hongjoong closes his eyes and tries to relax until the pair in question return. Minseok puts cups of hot tea into his and Tamryn's hands during their wait. The silence breaks when there's a shift in the room's air pressure and a soft pop.

"Welcome home," Minseok greets without looking up.

In the entryway stands the two men from the deli; they wave to Minseok as they take their shoes off and enter the main area. Before they can greet the others, Hongjoong stands, rounds the couch, and stalks up to them.

"What did you two do? I could feel your magic all the way from the mountains!" A growl follows his words as he jabs his finger at them.

The taller of the two immediately steps forward to block the other as the lavender hair one snaps back. "What's with the third degree?"

The other glares at their leader. "And what magic? Nico and I were on a lunch date, nothing magical about it."

"Yeah, Rey wasn't even that romantic today," Nico jests, to which Rey reaches back and smacks his chest as he laughs.

"I'm serious, you two," Hongjoong crosses his arms. "There was a pulse of dark magic, *strong* dark magic. Can you say with certainty that it was not you?"

"Yes," they chorus with wary looks.

A knife clinks as it's set on the counter, and it breaks the trio's focus. They turn their attention to the kitchen as Minseok wipes his hands on a towel.

"Hongjoong, you can't just go around declaring it was dark magic," he scolds, "they obviously didn't do it, but how can you be sure it was dark magic?"

"It was my type of magic, or something Azrael's coven would have used. You two," he gestures to Rey and Nico, "know some demonic-based spells from your upbringing, and you were in town. I need you to promise me you didn't use magic today."

"None!" "Absolutely not!"

"Then," Hongjoong's shoulders tense, "that means we have a new witch in town. It's been, what? A few years since any witch has been here?"

Tamryn sets his book down and stands up. "It was one of my coven witches a few years back," he walks over to join them. "They wouldn't be back though, they aren't smart enough to know what you did."

"Should we be concerned?" Minseok asks.

"Maybe?" Hongjoong scratches his head.

Rey and Nico stare at each other; they share a silent conversation that the others can't translate.

Hongjoong waves at them. "alright, you two, what's up?"

They look at Hongjoong, then back to each other. After a minute of them communicating through gestures and facial expressions, Rey blurts out, "But she couldn't be. She looked so normal!"

"I'm sure we seem normal to others," Nico counters.

Rey sighs.

Nico turns and explains, "We ran into this girl at our usual place. She was new in town and looking for a place to stay."

"Like a hotel?" Minseok asks.

Rey shakes his head. "No, a place to rent for a while. She's staying in town."

Tamryn lets out a long sigh.

"Give me all the information, who she talked to, what she looks like, I'll find her," Hongjoong says. "I'll check to see if she's a witch, and if she is, I'll take care of her."

They give him all the information they remember as he puts his boots back on and throws on a coat. He then leaves and makes his way through the woods to town. He keeps one hand at his side and focuses his magic to find traces of this new witch. He takes a few moments to find a hint of new magic or essence. It isn't until he's by the deli where Rey and Nico saw her he gets faint traces. He walks around for a while before he picks up a solid scent to follow. The trail leads him to the local grocery store, and once inside, the magic pulses from a single source among aisles. He tucks his hands into his pockets and uses his feline abilities to stalk through the aisles with slow, quiet steps. When he rounds the corner of one aisle, he stops at the sight of the witch the magic is trailing from.

Red hair, pretty, short, all the details the huskies gave him check out. Her magic is potent; he makes his way towards her on light feet as he waits for an opportunity to approach. Then she goes for a box on a shelf she can't reach on her own.

"Here, let me," he says as he reaches over her to grab the box. When she turns to him, he flashes a smile.

"Thank you," she says after she looks him over.

He tilts his head. "You must be the new girl. College road trip, right?"

"I am." Her smiles is pleasant, but he can see a pinch to her face. "I guess news spreads fast in a small town."

He resists the urge to roll his eyes by laughing. "It does," he hands her the tea, and as soon as their fingers touch, he feels a surge of energy; his smile widens. His magic courses through him, and he casts a silent spell.

"It's such a small town that most people forget it's even here." It rolls off his tongue with practiced ease. His magic pulses and works to contort her mind through the slight touch of skin. He grins and waits for her body to freeze and her eyes to glaze over.

Then she pulls her hand back.

A bucket of ice water drops on his head, and his eyes widen. Something akin to fear stirs in his gut as he watches her place the tea in the cart. His ears buzz, and he looks at his hand, then back at her as she slips. He catches her and holds her wrist as he tries again, but she brushes it off once more and leaves.

Once she's out of sight, he turns back and locates a random human standing alone. He makes sure the coast is clear before he approaches the man and places his hand on his arm.

"Sorry to bother you, but you promised you'd give me five dollars." The lie comes with ease, and the magic courses through him once more.

The man's eyes glaze over, and he gives a cheerful response before he pulls out a five-dollar bill and hands it to Hongjoong. Relief is only momentary, as it doesn't explain the mystery the new witch has created.

He returns home in record time. Concern evident, but he tries not to let it show as all seven of his coven members greet him. Each pair of curious eyes makes him more nervous; a hush falls over the room that sets him on edge as he rubs the back of his neck. Still unsure of how to explain what happened, he takes a minute to think.

Minseok is the first to approach him. He places a hand on his arm, which pulls him back from his head.

Hongjoong looks at Minseok. "She was immune to my powers. How can a witch be immune to mind control?"

A muscular witch with styled fire-engine red hair turns from his spot at the dining table, which looks small compared to his size. "Did she feel like a demon specialist? I worked up an immunity to your magic, but that's only because we both study demonology."

Hongjoong shakes his head. "Her natural magic is dark, but less like it's meant to be and more like it's tainted."

"So similar to mine?" Tamryn asks.

"Exactly, but that still wouldn't make her immune to my magic." He turns back to Minseok, "She could be dangerous, but I'm not sure what her affiliations are."

"Maybe we wait and see, examine her from afar," another witch, of similar stature and height as the red haired one, but with sandy-brown hair that falls around his ears says. "She doesn't know we're witches, right?"

Hongjoong nods.

"That's perfect, Joshua," the red-haired one claps his hands. "We just watch her, study her and see if she's a threat. If she's not, then we leave her be. No harm."

Minseok smiles. "I like that idea, Azrael. I can do a health check and see if there's any dark magic inside her we should be concerned about. I think," he tries to stem the fear he senses in Hongjoong by saying, "if she was here for us or to harm witches, she would have known what we are."

The rest of the coven agrees.

"Come on," Minseok takes Hongjoong's hand and walks him to the kitchen, "you are going to drink a cup of hot tea, eat something, and then go sleep. As for the rest of you," his gaze hardens, "don't bother him and don't worry too much about the witch, we'll look after it."

Nico raises an 'okay' symbol as their youngest, Hatawa, a clearly Native American witch with short black hair, dark skin, and prominent muscles snickers from his spot next to him on the couch.

"Alright, mom, you and dad got this!" Hatawa gives them a thumbs up, making Hongjoong laugh and Minseok blush as he busies himself with making the tea.

As the sun rises the next day, Minseok wakes and bakes a few batches of muffins and pastries. He weaves his magic and herbs into each one to create a dry potion inside them, which will allow him to track vitals and magic. He then takes a couple of baskets from the pantry in the kitchen and fills them as each batch finishes.

The first person to rise is Rey, who sits at the dining table, still half asleep as he slumps down onto the tabletop.

Minseok picks up a muffin and a black tablet and sits next to Rey.

"Be my test subject," he says as he sets the muffin in front of Rey, who perks up.

"Free food from our best baker? Why, of course, I'll eat it," he takes the muffin as Minseok smiles at him.

When Rey eats the muffin, notifications begin to appear on the tablet. Minseok lets out a sigh of relief as he opens the report and looks over the results.

"It says you're still lacking the herbs I keep telling you to add to your food," he says.

Rey shrugs and mutters, "They make everything taste weird."

Minseok shakes his head. He lays the tablet down and rests his chin on his hand. "I'll let it go for now, but it looks like all the updates worked, so that's good."

Rey holds a hand in front of his mouth. "As for my energy levels, they should be lower than usual. I was up late with Nico."

Minseok's face wrinkles, and he opens his mouth when Rey quickly explains.

"No, not that, you freak," he rolls his eyes. "This whole witch thing is really bugging him, so I stayed up with him until he drifted off; used a bit of magic to help him fall asleep, so he'll be out for most of the morning."

"That's good to hear. This new witch's results won't be as quick as yours. I'll have to build her a profile on here."

"Don't you need a DNA sample to do that, though?"

"A simple handshake can take care of that," Minseok waves a dismissive hand and stands up. "At least I know it works."

For the rest of the morning, Minseok stays in the kitchen and finishes baking while he cooks breakfast for the coven as they all slowly wake up. Amid all the usual chaos of the coven's day-to-day life, Minseok makes sure Hongjoong is alright to watch the coven while he heads off to visit the new witch. Once he gets the okay, he takes the basket and sets off for town.

By this point, he's felt her magic on Hongjoong, so it isn't hard for him to find the trail and follow it to her home. At first, he stands across the street and examines the glamour she's laid over it; it's not as intricate as Tamryn's, but it is impressive.

He moves the basket behind his leg as he walks up and gently knocks on the door.

It takes a minute before the doorknob twists and opens to reveal the short red-haired witch. He flashes her a smile as her eyes study him.

"Hi," he holds out his hand. "I'm Minseok; I live in a cabin nearby. I heard Chase rented this cabin out, so I wanted to give you a warm welcome to Highlands."

"Thank you, it's nice to meet you," she shakes his hand. "My name's Lauren."

He lifts the basket and explains the gift as he puts his other hand in his pocket and presses it into a sheet of paper to collect her DNA. He feels terrible for lying when he senses that her aura underneath the darkness is sweet and soft. This is evident as he watches her face soften into a genuine smile, and he sees a hint of tears at the corner of her eyes.

"You didn't have to. This is too sweet!"

Smiling brighter, he says. "We don't get a lot of new people who stay here, so I thought," he shrugs, "why not."

"Thank you, seriously." She can't seem to wipe the smile off her face, and it melts his heart.

"You're welcome. I hope you enjoy it here." He takes his leave with the conclusion that she has a strong innocence under the darkness that hangs off her. He deduces her coven must be of a darker nature, but she isn't.

Upon returning home, he takes a seat at the dining table and inputs Lauren's DNA into the tablet and sets it aside as he waits for the results. He reads over the latest research papers on the mix of technology and magic to pass the time.

It's not until sunset that the notifications come in with Lauren's results.

The base results come through first. It states her health is positive, so he dismisses those and scrolls to the notifications about her aura. The dark magic is ever-present and prominent on the surface above her lighter aura. As well, her aura is low in power; she's weak, and her strength is diminishing.

Hongjoong is the first to realize what Minseok is up to. He joins him at the table and peers down at the tablet. "What's her verdict?"

"Very innocent." He slides the tablet over so Hongjoong can see it too. "The dark aura is just a coating; it covers up an abundance of good magic. It's a tough shell, though, and I think part of it is killing her magic."

Hongjoong sighs and reaches over to see the results himself, which brings a soft blush to Minseok's face. "Why would her aura be so low power-wise? From the looks of it, she's had an energy potion recently."

"She did, but it looks like it only refilled it, not re-powered it. Usually, we see these levels after major trauma or even during severe depression, similar to how we found Tamryn," he hesitates and taps his fingers on the table. "It is interesting how similar the two are. Where is he anyway?"

"Good question," Hongjoong leans back and looks around the room at the rest of the coven.

Both are aware everyone has been listening to them, so Hongjoong raises a brow as he waits for one of them to answer.

The youngest clears his throat. "He's out for a flight."

Minseok clicks his tongue. "And that means he went to visit her."

"I did," the sliding door in front of the dining table opens; Tamryn steps in. "I was in my animal form; she didn't know who I was, don't worry."

Minseok asks, "What did you learn?"

"She's creating a tracking spell; she mentioned something about a family tragedy."

"That would explain why her power is so drained." He moves the tablet back towards himself and scrolls through the results again. "As a healer, I don't think she is any concern. I think she's in more danger with how weak she's. If anyone comes after her, she wouldn't be able to fight."

"Then we leave her be," Hongjoong states. "We can monitor her, but other than that, we just leave her alone."

Lost

Over the next few days, a thick layer of snow blankets the town. Lauren tends to her herbs and makes sure they're safe from the snowfall. The rest of her free time is spent in the local library, where she sits and reads both mundane and spellbooks as she prepares for the tracking spell. Which takes more time than she had expected; the easiest part was setting up the brewing station. Most often, she sits in the living room and tests the different herbal mixtures for the spell. She still wears her mother's necklace and has her parent's photo set on the counter where she can see it, as a reminder of who this is all for.

It's almost a week since she arrived when she decides to contact Damien. They aren't the best of friends or even that close, but he's the only one in the coven she's had a connection with.

Astral projection is the easiest way for witches to communicate over long distances. Some covens have updated with modern technology, but her coven has always been more old school. The setup is simple: a circle of candles and salt, for protection, in a dark, silent room so there are no distractions. It's been a long time since she's done this, so she takes extra precaution by triple-checking the circle before she begins.

The moment she closes her eyes and her consciousness transfers to the spiritual plane is always unpleasant. The world turns dark, and cold seeps into her bones, which makes them ache. She pushes away the unpleasant sensations and focuses on Damien's aura. She locks onto it and follows it back to her coven's land. When she opens her eyes again, she finds herself inside Damien's room. She's only ever been in the simplistic room once or twice, but it looks no different: a bed, a dresser, and a desk are all that occupy the space. At the desk sits Damien himself, and his head jerks up as he senses her presence.

"Lauren," he flashes her a smile, one that seems off-kilter, "what are you doing here?"

Her astral form walks to him. "I wanted to see what happened since I left and tell you I was alright."

It's silent for a moment, then he laughs. He stares at Lauren in disbelief. "Wait, wait a second." He takes a minute to collect himself before he asks, "Why would you want to let me know how you're doing or that you're safe?"

Lauren blinks and tilts her head. "You're my friend? I thought you'd want to know."

A bark of laughter is his first response; he shakes his head. "Sarah is going to get a kick out of this."

A slight tremor of worry grows in the pit of her stomach as she waits for him to explain.

"Lauren, I was never your friend."

The words almost break her focus, her astral form wavers and flickers like a fading TV. Confusion and hurt dance across her face as she takes a step back.

"Damien, what are you," she lets out a breath, "what do you mean?"

"My mom," he starts with a grin, "and a few other parents decided you'd be too volatile if left alone. Of course, no one wanted to be friends with the outcast's daughter, but you alone and filled with hate would be dangerous to the coven. So, they paid me to be friends with you."

"Paid?" The word leaves a sour taste as she says it. "That's not-you were so nice all the time, you couldn't have been-"

"Faking it? Oh, I was in the beginning for sure, but by the end, you believed my annoying teasing to hurt you was friendly banter." She flinches away at the venom in his voice. "It's funny, really, because, here you are, coming to me when I'm the one in charge of the party hunting you down."

"I'm sorry, the party in charge of hunting me down?"

"Yeah! We were kind of hoping that maybe getting rid of your dad would solve our problems, but then we went to collect his evidence, we found it gone," he stands from the desk and walks towards her, "and the only person who could have taken it was you, his meddlesome daughter."

She stands and processes the information; the realization of how serious the situation is, causes her form to flicker again.

"Your dad was onto us. I'm sure you can understand why we're hunting you down for the information you now have, and since I was the closest to you, I'm the one in charge of finding you."

That shocks her back into reality. "So, you're all looking for me to make sure I don't take the information to The High Coven?"

"Exactly, and you," he waves his hand at her, "projected yourself right into my room. It isn't easy to track astral forms, but I'm sure you won't be a hard little kit to find."

A shiver runs down her spine as her stomach churns. She looks at him, but she doesn't recognize him anymore. With a sinister smile and evident joy from her fear, he's no longer the Damien she thought she knew.

"Did my friendship mean anything to you?"

"No." He answers with no hesitation. "You were a paycheck, and now you're a job, nothing more."

Tears brim in her eyes as her emotions win over her concentration. Damien's smile grows wider, then her concentration snaps, and she crashes back into her body.

Her skin is cold, and there's a hollow sensation deep in her soul. Even with the candles and the heater, she feels as if an icy wind has swept into the house. For a while, all she can do is sit numbly with tears pouring from her eyes. The emotions swirl and cloud her mind, drawing her deep into a black hole as it hits her.

She has absolutely no one left.

Heavy sobs and cries of anguish fill the house. She wraps her arms around her knees and pulls herself into a ball as she heaves and cries. In the back of her head, she knows she needs to leave the house and go somewhere in town so Damien can't track her, but first, she lets herself cry and feel every negative emotion, even as it drowns her and dampens her magic.

After a while, she pulls herself together. She collects her study material for the tracking spell and heads out. It's late afternoon and the cold air shocks her system and brings her tears to a halt. She wipes away the evidence, though if anyone were to look close enough, they would still see her red and puffy eyes.

The numbness doesn't leave. The snow and cold don't help ease any of the emotions clouding her mind, but she pushes them aside and hurries to the sanctuary of the library.

Inside, the lights are soft, and a blast of warmth greets her as soon as she opens the doors. It's quiet. There are barely a handful of people throughout the desks and shelves, but she ventures to the study area in the far back, where no one is likely to catch a glimpse of her spellbooks. As she takes her seat, she makes a silent note to be on guard with her spell muttering and to make sure her books are concealed since there's a group of boys a few tables away.

After a minute of sitting in silence, she pulls out her research materials, and opens them to where she left off. The page of her notebook is full of detailed notes and scribbles, while the books have marks throughout the margins. She stares at them as she taps the pencil on the page. She tries to focus on the material and not on Damien, but eventually, teardrops appear on the page, and she has to wipe her eyes with a shaky breath.

The chair across from her scrapes the floor; one boy from the lone group sits down. In trying not to cry, she didn't notice him get up - much to his friend's surprise - and walk over to join her. She looks up to find a shy looking man with light brown eyes and dirty blonde hair smiling at her. He looks hesitant as he folds his veiny hands together, and in a gravelly timbre, he gives a gentle, "Hi."

She responds with her own, "Hi."

The man looks down for a second and says, "You look troubled and like you might need to talk to someone."

"Oh," she blinks and sits up straight. "Is it that obvious?"

"A little," he laughs, "but I promise, it's not too obvious. I'm very good at reading people, and I know from experience that talking to strangers can be easier than talking to people you know."

She nods and taps her pencil faster as she bites her lip. The idea of dropping her sob story on a stranger doesn't sit right;

sharing anything with anyone other than her father never has.

The man seems to sense her hesitation and says, "I'm aware it's weird, but someone once did this for me," he steals a glance at the table of men, who she notices have their eyes on them, "and it helped a lot."

"That's fair, but," she trails off as the group turns away like startled deer.

"Don't mind them," he waves his hand, and for a second, she thinks she sees a spark, but he folds his hands back on the table. "They're nosy. Now, do you want to talk about it?"

She laughs and smiles. "It's not a big deal, really."

He raises a brow. "You're crying, so obviously, it's a big deal to you."

With a sigh, she relaxes back into her chair. "Okay, so I'm sure you know I'm the new girl in town on a college vacation, right?"

He nods.

"Perfect, short backstory covered. Well, I'm not popular back home, and I needed to get away, but I had this friend... he was the

only one who liked me, but I," she pauses
and looks from him to his friends. Humans.
She shifts her language, replaces her witch
vocabulary with human terms, and
continues. "I called him to tell him I arrived
fine, and that I was okay. It surprised him to
hear from me, like startled, and he asked if I
thought we were friends. When I said yes,
he laughed and told me we were never
friends, and our families literally asked him
to befriend me," the last part she says in a
rush as fresh tears slip from her eyes. "My
only friend and it turns out he was just
faking it all these years, and now I have no
one."

At first, the man is silent, his mouth
open as he stares at her. She doesn't look at
him, though, afraid she'll see pity or regret.
The silence stretches on until a pale hand
comes into her view and soft fingers grasp
her hand.

"That's shit," he says. "That guy? He's
an asshole, and you deserve better."

She laughs and uses her free hand to
wipe away her tears. "You don't even know
me."

He hums. "True, but I have this feeling that me and you are a lot alike. What I know," he squeezes her hand as she looks at him again, "is that if I ever meet this guy, what's his name?"

"Damien."

"Damien, if I ever meet Damien, I will punch him for you." She laughs again. "You'll find better people, trust me. I came from a shitty situation too, and I found a great family."

"Thank you," her soul feels lighter, and the man's smile brings a quiet peace to her heart. "Honestly, you're too kind."

He smiles and lets go of her hand as he stands up. "You're welcome; I hope you feel better. Maybe we'll meet again at some point, but for now, take it easy?"

"I will," she looks down but hastily looks back up. "Wait! My name's Lauren. Can I at least get yours?"

He hesitates and glances at his friends. He turns to her and whispers, "My name's Tamryn."

She repeats his name once with a smile before she lets him walk back to his table.

Tamryn strolls back to his coven and sits down as if nothing out of the ordinary has occurred. The other three at the table stare him down.

"I'm sorry, but," Nico, who sits across from Tamryn, asks, "what in the hell just happened?"

"Well," on Nico's right, Joshua clears his throat, "our shy and very antisocial coven mate just walked up to a total stranger and comforted them. I'm not sure if I should be proud or concerned."

"Concerned," Rey, who's across from Joshua, answers, "because that's like... Tamryn, seriously, what happened?"

Tamryn shrugs and focuses back on their study material while he uncaps his pen. "She looked distressed and sad; I couldn't just leave her be. Simple as that."

"No, no, no," Rey shakes a finger at him, "you have ignored plenty of distressed humans and witches. Why her?"

He ignores the question and reads aloud from the page they had left off on.

"Dude, no, you have to explain this!" Nico takes the book away and holds it away from the table. Joshua breaks into a fit of nervous laughter as Tamryn glares down at the empty space in front of him.

"Nico," there's an edge to Tamryn's tone, "focus on this study project, or I'm telling Hongjoong you broke his grandmother's vase and not a stray bird."

Nico pales, then he places the book back on the table, pulls out a pencil and declares they should get back to work without delay. Relived, Tamryn relaxes into his chair and begins to read from the spellbooks for them.

Alone; Together

Minseok and Hongjoong keep a close eye on Lauren. Tamryn runs into her a few times at the library; Rey and Nico run into her at the deli, but she suspects nothing. Hongjoong realizes she is not a threat to his coven, and he relaxes.

Lauren continues to test different mixtures and spells. Each and every one fails. Scorch marks across the floorboards around the brewing station showcase her failed attempts.

As the snowfall builds, so does the holiday spirit. The town becomes illuminated in lights and decorations. Thanksgiving comes fast. Despite it being a human holiday, most witches still celebrate it in their own way, unique to each coven.

Hongjoong's coven always has a large feast. Everyone takes part in the preparation, and after the food has gone, they play games and swap stories.

Lauren and her father would cook their own meal and spend the day in front of the

TV watching human movies. The rest of their coven had their own celebration, but they never joined in.

This will be her first Thanksgiving alone, and the thought reminds her of her father's horrific death sending her into a spiral as the day approaches. She sits on the couch, wrapped in a blanket, while her brain runs in circles with images of the train wreck stuck in her mind. In an almost catatonic state, she eats and continues her work, but most nights, she breaks down and cries until exhaustion takes hold. She wakes up and does it all again. On top of it all, the tracking spell isn't working, which adds fuel to her depression as she knows her coven is on their way. A part of her brain can't help but think she may not have long before she joins her father.

A firm knock on her door early Thanksgiving morning breaks her out of her head for the first time in three days.

She wipes her face to hide any traces of tears and runs fingers through her hair to tame it.

"Hold on," she calls as she waves her hand to create a glamour over the brewing station.

The bitter cold and snowfall sweep inside as the door opens. It makes her shiver as she pulls her jacket close. She looks up to see Minseok on her step; he's dressed in an oversized brown coat with a beanie to shield his head from the snow.

"Good morning, Lauren," his voice is too chipper for the stiff wind and early hour, but it brings a smile to her face.

"Morning, Minseok," she wraps her arms tighter around herself as she leans on the door frame. "What brings you over?"

"Well," he draws out the word before he, once again, pulls a basket from behind his back. "It is Thanksgiving, and I couldn't help but think of you being alone on a holiday usually spent among family. So, I had some extra food-again-and I really didn't want you to feel alone."

"You're too generous," she gladly takes the basket, "but I love this, thank you. It is weird being alone on the holidays, but I'm fine."

Even though she flashes him a genuine smile, she knows she is not okay.

"What do your roommates think about you giving away food?" she jests lightheartedly.

Minseok sucks in a breath with a playful smile. "There's two who love food more than each other, so let's not tell them I gave some away. I had to go out to buy more supplies for dinner anyway, so it was a perfect excuse."

"You really are too kind, thank you. Now go," she waves her hand back towards the road, "before it gets any colder. Your friends might be mad if you got sick on them; I can only guess you're their cook."

With a hearty laugh, he steps back and says, "I am, but on holidays they cook," he winks; she laughs behind her hand as he heads off into the snow.

As she steps back inside, she mutters a heating incantation to warm herself; she takes the food to the kitchen and places it on the counter. It's unusually warm, the basket seems to radiate heat, and she almost questions it but decides it's easier not to. Inside is an assortment of bread, turkey, and fruit. It's not a traditionally big Thanksgiving meal, but it's enough to warm her heart. She makes a mental note to do something nice for Minseok before she's forced to leave. The stray thought brings everything back; her moment of relaxation breaks.

"Just," she sighs, "focus on this gift and be thankful that at least some people in this world aren't trying to kill you. After today, I can start again on the spell, but for today let's just breathe."

With the help of warm home-cooked food and basic channels on the TV, she finally feels a small sense of calmness. Her energy levels back out, and she can sense her magic settle in her veins, no longer statically charged from stress and fear. Soon, it lulls her into a deep sleep, with no nightmares, just peaceful bliss.

The following day it's back to business as usual for the coven, until Hongjoong's loud, bellowing voice draws everyone's attention. As the members shuffle out of their rooms, they find Hongjoong and Minseok standing toe-to-toe in the living room. The shorter of the two is seething, so much so that sparks fly from his fingertips, and a dark red streak flashes through his eyes, all while Minseok stares him down with an unreadable and stoic expression.

"You not only took her food," Hongjoong states, voice rising in volume, "but you drugged her food?"

Minseok stands firm and crosses his arms. "I did not drug her food in the way you're taking it."

"Oh," scoffing, Hongjoong tosses his head back, "then please explain."

"I cooked the food, and I topped it with a sprinkle of two crushed anti-anxiety pills, which I give to you," he uncrosses his arms to jab a finger at Hongjoong. "So no, I did not drug her food in a bad way."

"And what," his voice raises an octave, "possessed you to do this?"

He tilts his head and crosses his arms again. "Which part?"

"Minseok!"

"I didn't want her to feel alone on Thanksgiving. She doesn't have her coven, and she's not in the best place mentally. She's no threat. Plus, look at her aura now," he walks over to the dining table and grabs his tablet. "Some of the dark magic I was concerned about has left. It looks as if the little boost I gave her let her real magic retake control. When she wakes up, she should feel better than she has in years."

Hongjoong gives a heavy sigh; the tension lifts as he shakes his head. "You care too much about stray witches."

Minseok flushes and taps the side of the tablet. "I know, but if I didn't, I wouldn't have you," he pauses, then glances away, "or the rest of this coven."

"Promise me if this happens again that you'll at least run it by me first, since I am the coven head?"

"Deal."

Silence follows as Hongjoong sits down. Minseok stares at him for a long second before he walks into the kitchen.

"Are mom and dad done fighting?" Hatawa calls out from the hallway.

Hongjoong laughs, which brings a soft smile to Minseok's face. "Yes, you baby, we're done fighting."

The rest of the coven, having been piled up in the hallway listening, comes around the corner together. Tamryn, with a book in hand, makes a beeline for the couch while Rey and Nico slink up to the kitchen counter and give Minseok knowing stares. Azrael places himself next to Hongjoong at the table and asks, "Are we going to continue to ignore her then?"

Hongjoong nods. "While her magic is like the type we've dealt with before, it isn't worrisome. She's a baby witch, just like us."

Azrael smiles, satisfied with the answer.

It's a while later, as all eight of them are situated around the dining room eating, that the air shifts. Azrael is the first to notice, back rod straight as his eyes glaze over. Hongjoong notices next. He sees Azrael's reaction and feels the hair on his neck stand. A loud knock resonates from their front door, and they all fall silent.

No one moves. No one makes a noise. Everyone turns to Hongjoong and waits for him to make a move.

He pushes back from the dining table and walks to the door. There's another round of knocks as he approaches. He pauses and motions for everyone to stay back. Then he places a finger to his lips as he turns to the door and pulls it open. "Yes?"

"Hello," a short male witch stands on the porch. "Sorry to barge in on your territory like this, but my coven is searching for a fugitive witch."

"Really," he takes a step forward, "in this area?"

"We've been tracking her, and this was the last location. Her name is Lauren Muldoon, and she's a highly dangerous witch, here's a picture," the witch holds up an old photo of the witch in question, which is the Lauren they've run into, but he plays naïve and takes the picture to get a closer look.

"Her? She doesn't look dangerous."

"She's a loose cannon, untapped dark magic we can't control. We tried to contain her, but she got the upper hand."

Hongjoong raises a brow at the choice of words.

The other witch pauses. "She, uh… she killed her father and almost killed a few other innocent coven members."

"And you know it was her?"

"Yes, she was the only one with her father, and they'd just had a fight. You see," he slows his speech, which makes

Hongjoong frown, "her dark magic comes out when she's angry. Dark fire magic."

Somehow, he holds back a laugh. Murder? Dark magic? Minseok would have seen that in her aura. "Well," he passes the photo back, "my coven hasn't seen her around here, and we keep tabs on unknown faces. Plus, I don't like accusatory covens who blame people without evidence," the witch opens his mouth to protest, but Hongjoong reaches forward and takes the witch's hand. "Now, my coven knows this town and everyone in it; we have never seen her, and no one like her has been here. Your tracking must be off, and this town is no longer significant. Tell your scouts that."

With a shove, the witch stumbles off the porch in a daze and heads back down the driveway.

Minseok rounds the corner, eyes wide. "Hongjoong! If that's her coven, you gave yourself away. They specialize in dark magic! They'll know a dark magic touch!"

"I know."

"You know?"

"Nico, Rey, Azrael," he walks past Minseok as the three addressed stand up, "go get Lauren."

Found

Across town, Lauren sits in the living room, once again testing a tracking spell. The spoon in the cauldron stirs the bubbling lavender liquid. She holds one of her many books in her hands; the rest scattered around, and in her lap sits her notebook, which is open on a page covered in chicken scratch notes and blacked-out failures. With a groan, the book slips from her fingers and flutters to the ground.

"Work, work, work," she repeats under her breath as she grips her mother's necklace. She shifts up to her knees, takes the spoon from the cauldron, and then holds the necklace above. "With magic here to cast, seek what there is left to find, and show me the traces long since passed," the necklace stops moving, hanging straight down as the potion boils. The necklace moves in a slow circle, and just as she thinks it is going to work, the necklace jerks and the brew dies out with a puff of black smoke.

Even though she wants to scream, she sinks back onto her heels and sighs.

"Attempt twenty-seven," she grabs a pencil and looks to the notebook, "closer to complete, but still cannot give a direction. It achieved actual movement. Maybe too much sage. Lavender amount seems fine."

A silence falls when her hand stops. She takes a deep breath and looks over her notes.

"I'm so close," she bites down on the end of the pencil. The last ingredients and amounts dance in her head as she tries to figure out which ones to change for the next test. But then a heavy series of knocks shocks her out of focus. She sets everything down and stands up. As she walks to the door, she asks who it is and fastens her mother's necklace back onto her neck.

The chill air cuts through the house as soon as the door opens; it sends chills down her spine as she curls to stand partially behind the door. On the front steps are two familiar faces, with one unknown tall figure looming behind them.

"No time for formalities," the shortest of the three says, "we've known you're a witch.

We're witches. We are a small ragtag coven, and yours is after you. We're going to hide you for a short bit, and you're just going to have to trust us."

"I," she shakes her head and opens the door wider, "wait, hold up, there's an entire coven in this town?"

He rolls his eyes and repeats, "small ragtag coven," then he pushes his way inside. "Azrael, I need you to make this place look like she left in a hurry. They'll trace her here, and we need to make it seem like she left already."

The tall one follows him. Before she can figure out what to do, the third man steps inside and wraps an arm around her shoulders as he turns them to walk inside.

"Grab whatever you need that's important," the short one says, "but keep it small."

The way he orders her around hits a nerve; she shoves the one holding her and backs away towards the kitchen. "No, one of you explain this to me clearly! Who are you, and what do you know about my coven?"

The short one takes a deep breath as he pinches the bridge of his nose.

"Listen," the one who had his arm around her holds his hands up, "we mean you no harm. My name is Rey, this is my boyfriend Nico," he gestures to the short one, "and our coven brother Azrael. Since you came to town, we've known you were a witch, but we keep our coven hidden for purposes that you don't need to know. You didn't seem like a threat, so we left you alone."

"Then your coven shows up in town, one of them knocking on our door asking about you," Nico looks down at all the papers around her cauldron. "Our leader seems to want to help you, so he needs us to hide you while your coven gets put on a false trail. So," he glares at her, "grab what you absolutely need, and let's go."

"But-"

"No."

"Hold on-"

"No."

"Could you just-"

"Do you want your coven to find you?"

Lauren clams up. After a minute, she gives a reluctant nod in understanding. "Fine, let me collect some things," she heads off to her room and grabs her satchel, her father's documents, and collects her notes from the living room and places it all inside the satchel. The last item she packs is the photo of her parents. With her bag situated and slung over her shoulder, she turns back to them.

"Azrael," Nico looks over the rest of her things, "don't make it look like she was robbed but make it seem like she was in a hurry. Return to the coven house once you're done. Rey, you're with me and her," he steps forward and takes Rey's and Lauren's hands.

Lauren feels the all too familiar pull of being teleported. It's fast teleportation, but even so, when they land, she rips her hand away and stumbles onto the snow-covered forest floor. Coughing, she fights off a wave of nausea that brings back sharp memories of the last time she was teleported. For a second, she sees her father's smiling face at the train station, but then she shakes her head to erase it and forces herself to stand.

"That's got to be the worst someone has reacted to teleportation," Nico eyes her as she looks around.

"Where are we?"

"Just outside of town," Nico turns and walks over to a pile of snow as he snaps his fingers. Steam rises, and in a momentary burst of flames, the snow melts to reveal a wooden trap door. "This is an old storage place we use, but you can stay here until your coven leaves."

Rey guides her over with a hand on her back. "Don't unlatch the door for anyone. I have a special spell placed on the lock, so Nico and I are the only ones who can open it from the outside. We'll come back for you once your coven is gone."

She eyes the door while saying, "So I just have to trust you guys? I've only seen you around town a few times, and I just found out you're witches!"

With a grunt, Nico pulls open the door and holds it. "Yeah, I know. I'm still confused why we're helping, but we aren't cruel. Even if I'm annoyed, your coven seems like the bad kind, and we don't let innocent witches fall prey to them until we know the complete story."

"Which you will tell us when we take you back to our coven home, for now though," Rey gestures towards the cold underground bunker, "wait here, and you'll be safe."

She hesitates. Snowflakes swirl around them and twist in the wind as they sink into the dark bunker.

"We promise, we aren't here to hurt you," she looks back to meet Rey's eyes. They hold each other's gazes for a heartbeat.

"Okay."

With careful steps, she descends into the bunker and mutters a fire spell. The flame illuminates the small dusty room. There's nothing inside but a twin bed and cabinet against the concrete wall on her left. She holds the flame close as the door closes behind her, then takes a deep breath and sits down on the bed. The springs creak in protest and the cacked dust at her feet doesn't budge as the tips of her shoes slide against the floor. She glances at the cabinet, noting that it's sparely filled with pots and books, before turning back to the empty wall in front of her as she toys with her mother's necklace and waits.

Without the sunlight or any sound other than the occasional gust of wind, she isn't sure how long she spends there. A flash of light ignites the door, and a cascade of warmth floods the bunker; the lock clicks, and the hatch opens. This time, she doesn't hesitate to step out and welcome the chill air and heavy snow.

They don't speak. Rey gives her a tight smile as Nico hides the bunker once more, then he takes their hands and teleports them once again. Lauren is prepared enough to stay on her feet once they land, but she pulls her arm from Nico's grasp as she inspects the quaint living room they're in. There's no one but the three of them there, and she puts distance between them as she sidesteps towards the couch.

"Hongjoong!" Rey calls out, one hand cupped over his mouth. He turns to Lauren and gestures to the couch. "You can sit," and she does.

Two men enter the room and come over to greet her.

"Minseok?" The man in question gives a small grimace as he follows the other witch, whom she also recognizes. "And you're the weird dude from the store!"

"More importantly," Hongjoong waves Rey and Nico to leave as he stands in front of her, "you are a runaway witch whose coven is trespassing on our land."

"I didn't mean for them to find me," she lets herself sink into the couch as Minseok takes a seat beside her. "But, um... thank you."

It's silent for a minute. Hongjoong stares at her.

Minseok leans forward and rests his elbows on his knees. "You're welcome," he glances at Hongjoong. "Don't mind our leader. We just don't want trouble for our coven."

"Exactly, so all we need to know is where you need to go. That way, we can get you headed in that direction before your coven figures out. We tricked them."

"We rarely help your kind," the voice makes Lauren jump. She looks over the couch to see Nico in the hallway. Minseok mutters, "I thought we agreed we would handle this," as he turns to him.

"My kind?" she asks with a slight stutter.

"Demonic magic wielders," he waves his hand and rolls his eyes as if it's obvious.

"Oh," her shoulders drop as she looks down. "To be honest, I only recently found out my coven was a dark one. I uncovered all these documents too," she pats the satchel which she's placed on her lap.

"See, I told you she probably didn't know," Minseok shoots a glare to Nico as he slinks back around the corner and disappears.

Hongjoong steps forward to gain her attention. "What documents?"

Still unsure about them, she hesitates and grips the satchel. "My father figured out what magic our coven was using and what they truly valued more than the High Coven's codes. He tried to contact the High Coven, but our High Priest wouldn't allow it, and they killed my father. That's why I'm on the run," her knuckles are white, hands shaking as her words falter. "I need to get these documents to the High Coven. My coven needs to pay for their crimes."

"Wait, wait," Hongjoong up his hands. Confused, he says, "Your coven can't have a High Priest in it. That's not—that's not—no just, no."

"But... why?"

"To become a High Priest, you have to denounce your own coven, leave them behind, and physically leave the coven to join the ranks of the High Coven," he lets out a frustrated breath. "You can't be a High Priest and still be a part of a coven, let alone running it!"

"Oh, well, see, they didn't teach us that in school," she grows even more hesitant as Hongjoong's anger grows. "High Priest and Priestess Kensington told us they handle all High Coven communications and to come to them with any need. The two of them run the entire coven."

Hongjoong growls and kicks the coffee table; it slides towards Minseok and narrowly misses him as he swings his legs out of the way. With a shout and a burst of black and red sparks, Hongjoong storms out of the house.

It's silent for a moment before Minseok sighs. Once he's placed his feet back on the floor, he turns to Lauren. "Sorry about our leader; he is passionate about the High Coven and what they do for our covens. He's wanted to join their ranks since he was young."

Lauren blinks and tilts her head. "But they don't do much for covens. Our coven was told they try to let coven's figure things out on their own."

Minseok scoffs.

"My dad was told they wouldn't bother with little covens. He said they looked down on us."

He heaves a sigh and shakes his head. "That's not how the High Coven is at all; they care. In my coven," he steals a quick glance at the door and speaks softly, "my original coven, that is, they were there almost once a week at one point. They were trying to keep my coven heads in check, make sure they weren't abusing our women as they had been."

"Exactly," Lauren jumps as Hongjoong comes back inside. He closes the door and shakes the snow from his hair, "and to be a part of the coven, you have to study and train. Like I have," he walks back to Lauren's side of the couch. "Alright, so, you have evidence against your coven?"

"Yeah, I collected all my dad's documents before I ran away. As soon as I realized my coven had been killing people," she pauses, swallows back a wave of bile, and then continues, "and doing dark magic, I wanted to find the High Coven, but I didn't know how to without the High Priest. So, I've been trying to find my mother to see if she would know, but she left shortly after I was born. I've been trying a tracking spell on this necklace," Hongjoong and Minseok both look to the pendant around her neck, "but I'm still a novice, so I haven't been able to find any trace or trail."

"Wait," Hongjoong holds up his hand, "back up," he looks to Minseok, then back to Lauren. "They didn't even teach you how to ask for guidance? How to call on a High Priestess to gain some form of divine guidance?"

"No, we were to go to our High Priest and Priestess of our coven."

She hears Minseok sigh as Hongjoong closes his eyes and grabs his hair. He groans as he tugs on the strands. He then covers his face as Minseok reaches a hand out to rest on his arm. "Breathe," he murmurs and rubs his arm. It takes a few more seconds before Hongjoong calms himself down, and he nods as he opens his eyes again.

"What you are supposed to be taught," he says through his teeth, "is to pray to them."

"It sounds weird because we're witches," Minseok chuckles with a friendly smile, "but if you close your eyes and ask for the High Coven and tell them you're seeking guidance for an issue, they'll come to you."

"Not in their physical form, though," Hongjoong clarifies, "secrecy is huge in the High Coven. No one even knows the exact location of the High Coven, so more often than not, they'll astral project to you."

Lauren sighs. "That's how my coven traced me. I was trying to contact a–" she stops and sighs, "an old coven member, and he used demonic tracing to find me."

"We don't have much time," Minseok sits forward, "your coven will come back soon."

"These documents are important," Hongjoong sighs and looks to Minseok. They share a silent conversation. "I'd rather just send you on your merry way, but this is different," he turns back to her. "I know you're all listening in, so listen close. Lauren, we have to protect you; you have evidence that could help bring charges against corrupt covens. Which would be amazing. And we want to—no, we need to get those documents to the High Coven. Do you guys understand?"

The rest of the coven shuffles out from the hallway. Lauren does a quick headcount and pulls her satchel closer as she realizes how many members there are. Her eyes skirt across their faces, noting the few she's seen in town. They all seem hesitant. One, in particular, looks agitated, and it takes her a second to realize it's Tamryn. Her eyes linger on him before she turns her attention back to Hongjoong.

"I hate to ask you all to uproot everything, this is our whole lives, and the we've had a lot of good luck, but this," he gestures to Lauren, "is what we've been looking for; we finally have it. A way to bring all our covens to justice."

They whisper amongst themselves. Hongjoong walks over to listen to them, leaving Lauren and Minseok on the couch. She takes the time to process the situation.

"Is this a huge problem," she asks, "are there more covens like mine?"

Minseok looks at her for a long second, "Yes. They've been growing in numbers and working to break down the High Coven. They want to turn back to the old times and bring witches back to the days before the Salem event. Dark magic, bad laws, and chaos. Your coven is probably on the list."

"The list?"

"A list the High Coven has of covens that are a part of this new uprising, they're keeping a close eye on them. Tamryn and Azrael, the one off to the side and the tall one with red hair," she steals a glance to locate Azrael and put the name to a face, "their covens are near the top of the list from what we know."

Hongjoong claps his hands together as he walks back to the couch.

"We've all agreed to help, Minseok. You're okay with it, right?"

"I promised I'd always stick by you," there's a soft smile on his face, "plus I'm your healer; you need me."

"Fair enough," he rolls his eyes.

"The thing is we aren't all keen to help you in particular," Nico steps forward, "keep that in mind. We're more concerned about getting the documents to the High Coven so we can help our coven."

"That's comforting," she mutters as his harsh energy makes her shrink.

Minseok shoots him a warning glare.

"Well, if we're doing this, should I call a High Coven member for guidance? My tracking spells using my mother's necklace have not worked. It's too old, and she left too long ago, so I have no idea where to start," she explains.

"Yes, we'll start with you calling on a High Priestess. Minseok and I will be with you as you do this, so we know you aren't keeping anything from us," he turns to the rest of his coven. "This time, please, just go wait in your rooms and stop camping out in hallways. Let me and Minseok handle this," there's a protest from Rey and Nico, but after a good long stare from Minseok, they concede and retreat with the rest.

High Priestess

Once they're alone, Hongjoong takes the seat beside Minseok. Lauren asks him to reexplain how to contact the High Priestess. He seems annoyed, but Minseok lays a gentle hand on his shoulder, and he calms down. As nicely as he can, he goes over the process again. Minseok jumps in to clarify when he sees her face twist in confusion at points. Lauren then stands and moves to the open space in front of the repositioned coffee table. She sets her satchel aside and sits crossed leg on the floor as the two stay on the couch and watch her intently.

"Just speak to the High Coven, ask for guidance," she repeats to herself as she places her hands, palm up, on her knees, and closes her eyes.

The house falls still.

Minseok holds his breath and keeps his eyes open for an apparition. Lauren concentrates, repeats the phrase, "I don't know where to go, and I need the High Coven's guidance to find my way," inside her head on loop. She closes her eyes as she fights back pointless thoughts and forces herself to concentrate with a deep breath. She stays there for an undeterminable amount time and tries to be patient.

"She's here," Minseok says as he lifts his head from where it had fallen to his chest.

Lauren releases the tension in her body and opens her eyes to search around. For a second, there's nothing different. Then the air near the dining room table shimmers, and a statuesque figure in a long white robe appears. They walk towards the glimmer as it fades to reveal an older female witch whose black skin seems to glow, a telltale sign that she isn't physically present. Hongjoong's on his feet in an instant, Minseok close to follow.

"By my stars," the woman smiles, she tosses her dark red hair off her broad shoulder as she looks down on to Lauren, "it really is a lost coven child who has called upon us," she turns to the pair standing together, "and hello again, Hongjoong, Minseok."

"Of course, it would be you." Minseok gives a soft laugh.

"It's good to see you, Tamara," Hongjoong echoes his sentiment.

Lauren pushes herself back to her feet and puts her satchel back on before asking, "What do you mean, lost coven child?"

"You are not a coven member I recognize," Tamara motions for everyone to sit down. "Over the years, covens have disappeared into the shadows, shrouded from our vision and removed from our books. Tell me, dear, who is your coven leader?"

"His name is Kensington."

"Ah, now that was one of the first covens we lost. Interesting," she pauses as she looks at Lauren. "So, my dear, why have you called upon us?"

The High Priestess's scrutinizing gaze makes her want to hide. Still, she swallows her nerves. "My coven is full of dangerous witches, ones willing to kill their own blood to make sure no one contacts the High Coven. I have evidence to prove their wrongdoings and their location," she opens her satchel and pulls out her father's research. Aware that Tamara can't touch anything in her astral form, Lauren lays out the documents on the coffee table so she can read the important ones. "Some of these documents I don't even understand myself, but my father has been gathering evidence since I was a child."

Tamara is quiet as she looks at the documents. Her eyes rake over them all; Hongjoong and Minseok take the time to study them as well.

"This is vital information," Tamara says after a while, still looking them over. "This is what we have been looking for, what we have been needing."

Hongjoong sighs in relief, "I'm sad I never found it myself, but my coven has their own testimonies for other covens. We need to get these to you, we need to get to you." She looks away as Hongjoong leans forward into her field of view. "How do we do that?"

Tamara stares at him for a second, then smiles. "Similar to what I told Nico and Rey once upon a time, you already have the tools needed."

"Me?" Hongjoong's face twists, looking at Minseok in confusion.

"No. Well, yes and no," Tamara steps back from the documents, motioning for Lauren to put them away. "You have the tool, but she is the one who has to use the tool."

"Ah!" a lightbulb goes off as Hongjoong's eyes widen. Minseok now takes on the confused expression. Hongjoong hops to his feet and dashes from the room in a blur. He returns in no time with an old, worn compass in his hand.

Lauren has no idea what it is, but Minseok recognizes the item. "The compass, I thought it didn't work?"

"Well," he looks a little guilty, "I said it didn't, but it does. It's dark magic. Magic I've avoided, but it was given to my mom on her first day in our coven. A gift, a compass that will guide her to what she desires most." There's a bitter taste to those words as he glares at the object. "It's only supposed to work for certain witches, though he was vague about which ones could use it and which couldn't. It works for my mother and me, but no one else."

"And you don't use it because of the dark magic?" Lauren asks.

"Yeah," he walks over to her seat, "I've been trying to separate myself from as much dark magic as I can since Minseok and I left our coven, but you still have a lot of dark magic in your veins; from your coven."

"I hate to break it to you, Hongjoong, but that is not dark magic," they all turn to Tamara. He opens his mouth to protest and call her bluff, but she silences him, "That is pure divine magic radiating off it, and the witch who gave it to your mother must have been a divine witch. They are very rare."

Hongjoong turns it over in his palm, "I was so drawn to it though. I could have sworn a dark witch charmed it," as he turns the compass back over, the arrow spins and points at Lauren. Hongjoong can't help but laugh. "I can't even think of what I want most right now. I really don't know," he tosses it to Lauren.

She fumbles but catches it. Her heart rate picks up as she holds it in her palms.

"Think of what you want most," Tamara instructs. "I already know what you want. You are on the right path."

Her words fade with her astral form and leave the room silent.

"Always cryptic," Minseok grumbles.

Lauren looks at the compass. She needs to get the documents to the High Coven, but her mother still comes to her mind. All she can picture is her mother's face. The High Coven needs her, but so does her mother. The compass points true north before it spins, calculating. It spins for a good minute and then stops; the arrow points west.

"Minseok," Hongjoong's face breaks out into a wide grin as he stares down the compass, "get a map."

They spread the map across the coffee table as the rest of the coven joins them. With the map out and only a single direction to go off, they deliberate the probable location of the High Coven. The space between them and the western coast leaves many options to explore. As the rest of them discuss possibilities, Lauren situates herself at the dining table with Minseok, who seems uninterested. In his hands are her documents. He asked to read them over while the rest of the coven set up the map; she decided he was the most trustworthy of the coven, so she has no fear of him reading over her father's work. While he sits and reads, she continues to examine the mysterious compass. No matter how she turns it or what she thinks about, it always points west, though not directly west. For the brief moment, before Hongjoong ran to get the coven, it seemed to point west, but the arrow rests just above the west marker.

"Memphis? Los Angeles? Vegas? It could be any of these!" Azrael tosses himself onto the couch and turns away from the map in defeat.

Hatawa looks over the map with Hongjoong, who says, "We could just head west, take the Amtrack to Los Angeles and test the compass at every stop."

"Taking the Amtrack from Memphis to Los Angeles goes north first and then west and south," Hatawa adds as he traces his finger over the vague path, "I've looked at it when I was thinking of taking the human way back home."

"Amtrack tickets for nine people; how could we even afford that?" Lauren muses to herself.

With a smile, Minseok says, "We have a rather large savings and a very persuasive leader, don't worry."

Even though he has the most calming presence, Lauren still feels weirded by some of his responses.

The bickering grows in volume and intensity until Hongjoong shouts to quiet them down; Lauren flinches.

"The best way is to take the Amtrack, as we said. This way, we can test the compass direction and see if we're heading the right way. To get to Memphis, though, we have to be careful. Lauren," she looks up to Hongjoong, "how well can your coven track people?"

"Very well, I mean, I was only in my astral form for a short time, and they still followed my trail," she says. "They're more than likely using a demon spell for tracking."

Hongjoong hums and turns to Azrael for any addition.

"That's probably right," he says. "From the time in my first coven, I learned demons use magic and spells more powerful than ours. For some reason, their energy is stronger."

"It comes straight from a source." The way Hongjoong says this, with such certainty, makes the hair on Lauren's neck stand up, but Minseok explains Hongjoong studied demonology extensively in their coven. "We use magic that's filtered, but demons and divine beings pull straight from their own source. Doesn't mean it's better or superior, though, as we've all seen firsthand."

Nico and Rey send side glances to Lauren; Nico's is still harsh. She sinks back into the chair and clutches her necklace.

"So, they're skilled trackers," Minseok pulls everyone back on course, "which means Rey Is golng to have hls work cut out for him, and Nico can't teleport us anywhere for a while. The less magic we leave behind, the better."

Everyone agrees with him on that.

"Now, before we embark on this, I think there are a couple of things that need clarification," Nico says. "Lauren, your coven told us you are a dark fire magic wielder–" before he can even finish or ask her to clarify, she laughs.

The sound of her high-pitched laughter feels out of place in the static tension, but the idea of her being a fire witch is hilarious. With the sudden rush of emotions come a few tears, which she wipes away as they roll down her cheeks.

"I'm not a dark fire witch," she says after she calms down. "I'm not even a dark witch. My main specialty is telekinesis, the first magic I mastered, and my second would be nature and healing. My father told me I inherited it from my mother," she shakes her head. "I'm the furthest from a dark witch there could be."

"Another healer," Minseok's eyebrows shoot up in surprise. "Could be good to have two healers, given the circumstances."

"I've always been told it's good to have two," she adds, "in case something happens to one, the coven won't be helpless."

Nico scoffs, rolling his eyes as he crosses his arms. "That doesn't mean you're going to be good for us. And until I have proof that you won't pull some dark magic out, I'm not gonna trust you. Plus, Hongjoong tried to use dark magic on you, small mind control to get you to just leave this town, and it didn't work, so no, I'm not gonna trust you. Rey, come on," Nico stands up and pulls his boyfriend with him as he storms out of the room.

His angry rant leaves behind a charged silence. Minseok glares at the empty entryway, and Hongjoong mutters something under his breath before going back to the map. As he and Hatawa look over the map, Joshua rises from the couch and makes his way over to the dining table.

"If it's any consolation, I'm a truth seeker, and you don't seem to be lying," he says with a hesitant smile, "but please understand most of us have come from dark covens who did horrible things to us. You reek of dark magic even if you don't use it, which makes you a magnet for it. We just want to be safe."

"I understand," the words are watery. She blinks back tears as emptiness gnaws at her chest. "I'll let you guys handle everything. I'm going to sit on the porch for a bit. Come get me when we have a plan," she pushes back her chair and walks to the back patio door, keeping her pace even and calm to hide any hint of emotion.

As soon as the door closes, Minseok rounds on Joshua.

"What? I was just being honest. She should at least know where we stand," says Joshua defensively.

"I get that, but still! Can't you see she's in pain from all she's gone through? Obviously, you can, so don't answer," he raises his hand to stop him from responding. "Just be a little decent next time. We don't have to like her, but we don't have to be cruel either," he waves his hand for Joshua to leave and turns back to the documents.

From the couch, Tamryn and Azrael watch and listen. Hongjoong refuses to acknowledge anything and focuses on the map.

A few hours pass and Lauren is still on the porch. She's sat with her feet pulled up in one of the few chairs free of snow. Despite the bitter cold, she doesn't dare go back inside. A small part of her hoped for something good to come of this new coven. They had saved her after all, but once again, she's alone, and that thought brings back the numbness and heartache.

"At least I can find the High Coven," she says quietly to reassure herself of her that this is the right choice.

The sun falls. The porch light offers a soft orange glow to the landscape. When the door opens, the sun has gone, and the dim light is all that illuminates the area. Hatawa's head pops out. He looks at her and raises a brow as he notes the fresh snow on her. It hasn't melted, which gives away how cold she is. Without a word, she stands up, brushes off the snow, and follows him inside. The only person left is Minseok, who motions her over to the couch where he sits with a steaming cup of tea.

"Drink," he says as she sits down. He pushes the cup into her hands before she can stop him.

Reluctantly, she takes it. "Is there a plan in place yet?"

Minseok hums an affirmation but waits until she's taken a sip before explaining the plan. "We hike from here to Memphis, should take a week or less, but it's the safest way with our tracker–Rey–covering our trail. That way, we don't leave a single trace of magic. From Memphis, we take an

Amtrack to Los Angeles, and from there, we can use you and the compass to track the High Coven."

"Is there a backup plan?"

"Not yet, but Hongjoong and Azrael are working on it. Both of them have some expertise in demon magic, so they're the ones who know best how to work with your coven."

"Okay, and I just need to stay out of everyone's way, right?"

Minseok sighs. "Sadly yes, I wish I could say my coven will grow to like you, they might, but it'll take time. This will be a long trip, so just play it safe."

The tea starts to leave a bad after-taste. She places the cup down on the coffee table. "Can I return to my place until we leave?"

"No, Hongjoong wants you here where we can keep an eye on you. In the morning, I'll take you over to collect your things, but for tonight you'll be sleeping here," he pats the couch and gives her a reassuring smile.

The emptiness continues to grow with each word, but she holds in her panic and gives a quick nod. Someone approaches them with quiet footsteps; Minseok looks up and smiles.

"Ah Tamryn, thank you," he stands up and reaches over the couch to grab a blanket and pillow from him. "You can have these," he places them next to her. "Try to get some sleep; it's going to be a long week."

She doesn't look at either of them. They share a concerned look, but they don't press. They leave as they begin a hushed conversation. She waits until she hears doors close before she lets herself relax.

She doesn't bother making any kind of bed with the blankets; instead, she collects her satchel, reorganizes everything, and places it under her head on the couch, not wanting it out of reach. Despite everything they've done, even here, she doesn't feel safe.

Nowhere is Safe

When the sun rises, Lauren is already awake. She could only sleep for a few hours. The rest of the coven wakes up in stages, Minseok being the first. He offers her breakfast but doesn't ask how she slept. Once the rest of the coven wakes and eats, Hongjoong pulls them to the living room to go over the details of their trip. He draws their route out on the map to show everyone before he packs it away. Then he familiarizes Lauren with each member of the coven, but he doesn't mention what animals they are, and she doesn't push her luck by asking.

As the coven disperses to pack, Minseok takes Lauren back to collect her things and put the house back for the actual owner.

Before they head out, Minseok stops her and holds out a charm.

"What's this?" She examines it as she takes it.

"It's a heat charm. Not as sophisticated as the ones the rest of my coven has, but we're going to be hiking in snow and freezing temperatures. This charm will keep you mostly warm. I didn't have much time to craft it, and Nico, our elemental, wouldn't help," he grimaces.

"Well," she gives him a soft smile, "thank you anyway, I appreciate the gesture."

By the time they return to the coven house, everyone is ready. They head out with Tamryn's glamour and stay on the highway as they leave town, then change course and head west through the rough forest. Tamryn lets his glamour fall after they've walked far enough to be out of human sight. As they hike, Rey's hand emits a white mist that wraps around them and clears any trace of their passing, from footprints to snapped twigs and chunks of snow that fall off the bushes they push through.

The snow underfoot is packed tight from the constant snowfall. Clouds cover the sky above as they trudge through the forest, though it doesn't snow, and the glare of the sun gives them enough light even under the treetops. With the tree cover, not all the bushes have been pushed down by the snow, so they have to fight their way through and go around a few times, but they keep their course and continue west.

Lauren stays near the back and keeps a safe distance from them. From the back, she examines their dynamics. As far as she can tell, all of them are animals accustomed to forest environments, except for Hongjoong, who is sure-footed, but gets easily tangled in the thick brush. There are distinct pairs that stick together. Nico and Rey aren't surprising; Nico stays attached to Rey's side. Hongjoong and Minseok lead them; Minseok pulls out the map a few times for Hongjoong to consult. The others flit between each other, though Joshua sticks close to Tamryn, who initiates no conversation. Hatawa or Joshua glance back at her a few times to make sure she's still there, but they never approach her. She's a fox, she isn't likely to lose her footing or fall behind, but she wonders if they'd even help her if she did.

They continue until the moon is high in the sky, and then stop to create a makeshift camp so everyone can rest. Minseok makes dinner for everyone, which Lauren tries to refuse. Inevitably, though, she takes the warm stew and sits a few feet away from them to eat. The heating charm works well enough in the bitter cold, but she can tell the rest of the coven's charms are more sophisticated. They don't shiver or flinch from the cold. She does her best to hide this from them and not show weakness. It's bad enough she's an outcast, but she needs them, and she knows that.

They continue this pattern of eat, hike, stop, eat, sleep, and so on for the next few days. Lauren keeps a mental tally every time the sun rises to keep her on track. On the seventh night, they make their way into Memphis and head straight for the Amtrack station.

Hongjoong and Minseok buy the tickets while the rest wait outside, and by this point, winter has taken a firm grip on the south. Lauren can't hold the shivers back. She sits on a bench as they wait with her jacket pulled tightly around her. The heating charm has worn down and is barely emitting anything. She focuses her energy on creating some semblance of warmth. With her mind distracted, she doesn't notice one of the coven members walk towards her.

"Here," she jumps and looks up to find Joshua holding out his jacket. "We'll be on the train soon, but you look like you need this."

Unsure, she reaches out a hesitant hand and coughs to clear her throat. "Thank you." She puts it on and feels warmth return. She smiles and gives him a nod in thanks, which he returns.

Not long after, Hongjoong ushers them all into the station. For the most part, it's empty. The holiday rush won't be for another couple of weeks. The lack of humans makes the station seem colder, eerier as they pass through. Something heavy settles in Lauren's stomach, but she pushes it down as they board the train.

As soon as everyone finds a place to sit and the train moves, Hongjoong addresses them. "This is a ten-hour trip, to Chicago. Once there, we'll test the compass and plan our next move. For now, I suggest you all get some sleep."

Everyone heeds his advice and settles in. Lauren gives Joshua back his jacket and thanks him again before sitting in her own seat a few rows behind them to give them their space. It takes a while for her to relax, but eventually, the sounds of the train lull her to sleep.

Somewhere in the middle of the night, after the interior lights have turned off, and the landscape becomes a black blur, the noises of the train morph into something sinister inside Lauren's head. The wheels screech and smoke fills her lungs. Muffled voices surround her as she opens her eyes to find herself alone in the train car.

"I'm sorry, miss." She turns her head and looks into the eyes of a crewman.

Smoke pours from the windows of the door behind him, the fire flickers just beyond it. Then her father's voice shouts for her from within the flames. She jerks up and back, stumbling away as the smoke and fire rush towards her.

"You were a paycheck," Damien growls right into her ear, "and now you are a job, nothing more," his voice turns demonic, and she tries to run forward only for the fire to flash and grow brighter as it crashes into her.

A hand grabs onto her shoulder and rips her away. She jolts in her seat, the usual sounds of the train return, and there's someone next to her. She flinches away as they hold their hands up.

"It's just me," Minseok says from his spot, crouched next to her.

She wipes her face and finds tears are running down her cheeks.

"You were distressed and crying." He lowers his hands as he watches her with worry etched into his features.

"I'm fine," she sniffs and uses her sleeve to wipe her tears away, "just a nightmare, no big deal."

Minseok frowns.

When he doesn't leave, she gives him a tight smile. "I'm good. Go get some rest."

He hesitates, but reluctantly stands up and returns to the sleeping coven.

Alone again, she mutters a sleeping spell to block her dreams as she sinks into the seat and closes her eyes once more.

~

The train arrives at Union Station the following day. As the coven disembarks, a handful of them complain about being hungry. Hongjoong makes a plea to test the compass first, but their cries for hunger win out. They disperse in different directions in search of food, after they leave a marking spell on a bench, so they can find each other afterward. Minseok hesitates to follow Hongjoong and Azrael; he eyes Lauren with concern, but then Joshua steps up and wraps an arm around her shoulders, which makes her lock up.

"We'll take her to get food with us," he declares with a broad smile as Tamryn joins him.

"And we'll make sure she eats," Tamryn cuts in as Minseok opens his mouth. "Go check on your man."

Minseok's mouth snaps shut as his cheeks flush, but he turns and hurries away.

"Come on," Joshua eases Lauren forward and leads her to the food court.

Unsure how to take this, she tries to speak as little as possible and lets the two of them converse as she follows. When Joshua asks her what she wants, she answers and allows him to pay. They get their meals and walk back through the station. Lauren stays silent and enjoys their peaceful presence.

The heaviness returns, and the hairs on her neck stand up. She falters and stops dead in her tracks as she looks around.

"Lauren?" Tamryn turns to her, but she doesn't look at him.

Just across the open space stands Lauren's worst fear, Damien. Her blood runs cold, her heart rate skyrockets, and her bones freeze. Damien grins and waves to her as he makes his way leisurely towards her.

"Lauren," Joshua steps towards her and follows her gaze, "who is that?"

"Damien," as she breathes his name out, Tamryn's head snaps.

"That's Damien?" he asks.

She nods as her hands shake. Joshua takes her arm and pulls her behind him. Tamryn takes a more direct approach. With rage rolling off his shoulders, he drops the food in his hand, marches up to Damien, and pulls his arm back and throws a solid punch to his face. This breaks Lauren's trance; she yelps as she covers her mouth.

"Take another step," Tamryn growls, "I dare you."

Damien laughs. He lifts his head as blood drips from his nose. "I see you've got a protection squad now, huh? Feisty bunch."

Joshua's eyes darken. "You're not getting her or the information she holds. We're taking her to the High Coven, and neither you, nor your coven or the other devil-worshiping covens will stop us."

"Oh, on the contrary," he wipes the blood away, "all of you are on our hit list now. They've marked this entire coven as a kill on site. Of course, my dear coven mate," he flashes her a smile, "is the first target, but if you get in the way, no one's going to hold back."

Damien's persistent grin boils Tamryn's blood. He lunges forward and lands a few more punches before he rushes back and ushers Joshua and Lauren back to the rendezvous point.

"If he's here, the rest of the coven has to be," Lauren says.

"I know," Joshua nods, "we can't wait for an Amtrack. We have to get out of here now."

As they round the corner, they see the coven is already back. Once Minseok spots them, he stands at attention.

"They're here," Joshua shouts as they rush over. "We have to leave!"

"They have a kill on sight order," Lauren adds, "for all of us. I'm sorry."

"Don't," Hongjoong surprises her, "it's okay. We knew what we were getting into. We'll handle it. What's your compass say?"

She fumbles to open her satchel, yanks the compass out, and holds it tight as she waits for the arrow to stop. "South-west, mostly south."

"Okay, we're still on track for California then."

"Guys," Azrael calls their attention to a group of black-cloaked figures.

"Go!"

Everyone gathers their things in a rush and makes a break for the main entrance.

A thick layer of clouds covers the busy city streets in a shadowless light. Light flakes of snow sweep through the air and create a foggy haze in the distance. Rey takes the lead and guides them through the streets, doing his best to not draw attention as they move through the crowds. He uses the snow and fog to their advantage once they reach the outskirts and start heading towards the countryside.

The snow and fog thicken as they run. They ditch the paved and plowed streets for the untouched fields where the fog sits the heaviest. Rey covers their trail as they continue to move and Tamryn does his best to glamour them, but it isn't enough in their haste. As they trudge through the deep snow, Rey spots a line of trees ahead, but before he can call attention to it the cloaked figures materialize around them.

"Down!" Hongjoong screams as they fire spells at them.

They all drop until the magic dissipates. Nico jumps up and stretches his arms, sending out a gust of wind that knocks them all back and gives them enough time to move.

"Head for the trees! Once we have cover, we can fight back!" Rey shouts.

They follow Rey's order without hesitation. Lauren keeps up with them as best she can, darting into the trees and brush. The sounds of magic fill the woods.

She stays as hidden as she can and makes her way through the bushes.

"There's a river!" Tamryn's voice comes from above. "Head for the river, and we can cross!"

She takes a second to orient herself by listening for the sound of water. It's hard to hear over the fighting, and the smell of fresh snow covers the scent of the river, but it's there. Faintly she can hear the roar as she crouches next to a tree. She closes her eyes to focus on the sound and locate it.

"Lauren!"

An icy chill runs down her spine. Her eyes snap open, and she stands up to put her back against the tree as she looks up. Damien's demonic eyes emerge from the hill above her. The rest of the coven isn't close; she can hear them further down near the river. Damien stares her down with a menacing smile as she conjures a ball of energy for defense.

"I have waited so long for this," his hands spark, black flames swirl from them. "Being able to put you in your place and remind you where you belong. I wish I could've killed your father too, but at least I can kill you!" The flames morph into solid balls, that pulse with raw magic.

Panic overtakes her; she realizes there's nothing she can conjure to fight him. Everything slows as Damien throws himself forward. The magic coalesses into one solid mass and flies straight down the hill. The force of it shatters the trees in its path. Splinters fly in every direction as the heat melts the snow. She feels the heat before it even reaches her, and she throws up a shield of thick vines to block most of the debris, but it's not strong enough to stop the fire. As it draws closer, the vines burn up. It sears her skin, and she screams in agony as she tries to hold on. There's a roar in the distance as it closes in, and just as quickly as it came, it ends in a blur of heat and black fur.

Air leaves her lungs as the tree breaks under the pressure as a figure wraps its arms around her. It holds her close as they're thrown through the air, down another hill, and into a small dirt patch with the rest of the debris. The two muscular arms that hold her vanish as she rolls another foot before getting her bearings.

Everything is bruised and cut; there are burns on her arms and legs, but thanks to her savior, they are only minor. The fight still rages around them, closer and still just as active. As she goes to sit up, she hears a whine from beside her. Quickly turning, she finds herself looking down at a tiny cub. It howls in pain as it rolls over onto its side, revealing a couple of large slashes and bloody, burnt fur. It screams louder when she reaches for it, and for a second, she doesn't understand what she sees, who this is, but then it opens its eyes, and her heart stops.

"Hatawa!"

Broken

Hatawa's distressed howls of pain echo in the small space. Lauren's ears ring. His cries are the only noise that penetrates as she stares in horror. The cries grow in volume, and the sound of the battle returns in a rush as she scrambles to him. She casts a stitching spell and places her hands over the wounds; the skin slowly closes in a red patch, but the fur doesn't grow back. Once the blood stops seeping out, she presses her hands on the skin to seal the wound. Then, she picks him up and holds him against her chest as he pulls himself closer to her and buries his face into her neck as he whimpers and chuffs.

Her body shakes as she apologizes. "I'm sorry. I'm so sorry this happened. You shouldn't be hurt; your coven is going to kill me." The sound of someone above forces her to move. She focuses on the sound of the river and makes her way through the snowy underbrush toward it.

They break the tree line and slide down to a riverbank where the roar of the current greets them. She stops herself just short of a large ice shelf that connects the shoreline to a deeper part of the river. Some of the ice breaks off due to the rough waters and is swept away without resistance. As she tries to keep her footing on the slick bank, she spots the rest of the coven on the thin shore upstream. They're worn and beaten as they fend off their attackers. She makes her way to them, struggling on the icy rocks, but she keeps a tight grip on Hatawa to avoid dropping him.

Minseok is the one to notice her first. A split second glance as he throws up a shield to deflect a blast of magic. "Lauren! Where is," he turns to her but quickly trails off when he spots the wounded bear cub she's holding.

"I'm sorry," she blurts out as tears fall. "He jumped in front of me and took the hit."

Minseok reaches forward, his hand hovers over Hatawa's head for a second before he lets it fall to rest there. "Is he dead?"

"No! Gods no, he's alive. I did my best, but he needs a better healer," she sniffles. "You should take him."

"After we cross the river." He turns and waves for her to follow.

Hongjoong shouts orders at Nico above the sound of the river; Tamryn holds a force field in place to keep the witches at bay as they collect themselves. Amidst it all, Lauren can't focus. Blood rushes through her veins, and her heart continues to beat too fast; all she hears is Hatawa's whines and her ragged breaths.

Nico, who's barely standing, steps into the water and clenches his teeth as the cold seeps into his skin. He waves his hand, and the surrounding river calms enough for him to move freely. "Let's go!"

Someone guides Lauren into the water as they form a line and slog across the river. Tamryn takes the rear and holds a force field for cover. Once they're past the ice shelves and have to swim to stay afloat in the deep water, Nico allows the current behind them to return to its deadly pace. Azrael and Joshua send a few defensive spells to counter and deflect the balls of magic thrown towards them. It isn't until they're halfway across and half-drowned in ice water that the fire stops, and the witches retreat and regroup. With no more threats, they pick up their pace.

As soon as they reach the shoreline, everyone collapses.

The weight of their drenched clothes and exhaustion knocks them down onto the shoreline. Some move up to the snowy slope, leading into the trees; the rest lay on the icy rocks to catch their breath. Lauren holds Hatawa as she falls to her knees at the water's edge. By now, Hatawa's whines have quieted down. He only makes a slight snuffling sound as he lifts his nose to press into her neck. She doesn't register the affectionate gesture or notice the coven members. They watch her closely as Minseok walks over to her.

"Lauren?"

Her head jerks up as he crouches next to her.

He says nothing, just holds out his hands for Hatawa. At first, she hesitates, but then nods and lowers her head as she pulls him off her shoulder. Minseok takes him with care and thanks her as he examines his wounds. "You did good," he says, hand gliding over Hatawa's back. "Thank you for saving him."

She steals a glance at him but sees Hatawa and looks back at her hands, which are covered in blood.

"Hey, hey," this time, it's Nico's voice. He walks up to them, "you need to breathe, or you're going to pass out... ah shit." He crouches on her other side, and reaches out to grab her arm, but she yelps in pain as soon as he touches it.

She finds her arms burned, and the pain comes full force at this realization.

"Hold him," Minseok shoves Hatawa into Nico's arms and swiftly heals Lauren's wounds. "Hatawa is stable. I'll do some more healing sessions on our way to wherever we go next. He's gonna need a lot more healing before he can shift back. You," he runs his hand over the charred skin and lets his magic repair the damage, "will need bandages. These burns have magic in them. By shifting, Hatawa saved himself from burn damage."

"I'm sorry."

He pauses and takes a second to look at her. "It's okay. We chose this."

She shakes her head, "But you didn't choose this!"

"We did," Nico speaks up; he grabs a roll of bandages from Rey. "We weren't expecting your coven to be that strong, but we agreed to this. And if Hatawa jumped in front of such a strong magic blast for you," he looks to the cub, heaves a sigh, and says, "Then you have to be a good person, so don't beat yourself up about this."

"We'll figure it out," Hongjoong adds from where he sits. He's up on the hill, patching up the less injured ones. "Right now, we need to take five and gather our bearings."

They move into the trees and out of sight of the other shore. Tamryn sets up a makeshift barrier while Minseok and Hongjoong tend to everyone else. At some point, Hatawa begins to whine again until he's given back to Lauren, where he curls up against her neck. Nico eyes them wearily but stays by Rey's side. Hongjoong and Minseok check each other's injuries last as the unspoken question of 'what now?' hangs heavy in the air.

"Hatawa needs a healer," Minseok starts, "one much more skilled than me or Lauren. Combined, we both did amazing, but he needs more advanced healing to shift back."

Hongjoong sighs. "The only healer like that is my mother, and I really didn't want to go back there."

"I know," he rests a hand on Hongjoong's shoulder, "but if the compass points that way, it may be best. None of you know any other excellent healers, do you?"

Everyone shakes their heads.

Careful not to jostle Hatawa, Lauren reaches into her pocket and pulls out the compass. "Who wants to figure out which way is north for me? I'm a little mixed up after everything."

Rey lifts his hand into the air and hums for a second before he points behind them. She turns the compass to face north and waits for the needle to stop spinning. It lands on the southwest marker.

"Well," Hongjoong says, "my coven would be southwest of here."

Azrael raises his hand. "Sorry, but how do we get there? Getting to a train station from here is going to be hell. That coven is going to be crawling all over this area."

No one answers him.

"I could try to teleport us," Nico offers.

"Babe," Rey shakes his head, "teleporting this many people would drain you completely."

"If we got to an Amtrak station, I could rest on the way." He turns to Hongjoong. "Where's your coven again?"

"Just north of Vegas."

"Right, so I can rest. I'll be fine." Rey still looks hesitant but gives a small nod. "Where could we teleport to?"

They take a minute to contemplate and discuss. Hongjoong pulls out the original map, and Minseok points out the original route. Many cities are too far or not far enough, and some they've never been to before, which makes teleportation nearly impossible. After some back and forth, they agree to jump to St. Louis. Azrael takes out his phone and searches for pictures of the Amtrack station, then he gives it to Nico to study them.

"This will be risky," Nico comments.

"Options are sadly thin. Let's get all our stuff together." Hongjoong motions to their scattered bags and belongings.

Everyone collects their things and forms a circle. Nico instructs them to hold on to each other tightly; Hatawa digs his claws into Lauren's clothes. Hongjoong takes her free hand in his, and Nico places his on her shoulder with his finger on Hatawa's fur to ensure he doesn't get lost. With their hands linked and the connection complete, Nico closes his eyes and channels his magic.

The teleportation is drawn out. It pulls at every molecule of their beings and disorients them as they're pulled and stretched through the different plains of space. There's a moment of limbo where everything hurts, then like a rubber band, they snap back into their skin and crash down onto solid concrete. Nico's concentration breaks before they can reach the ground safely. He lands on his feet, but his eyes roll back, and his body slumps. Rey reaches for him as he falls and rolls, so they land without injury.

"Sorry," Nico groans as he curls into Rey.

"You did good." Minseok holds up a quick thumbs-up from his position on the ground with everyone else.

They take a few minutes to catch their breath before they head to the train station. Nico hangs off Rey's arm with Azrael and Joshua on their flanks. Tamryn stays by Lauren and Hatawa's side while Hongjoong and Minseok take the lead. The station is relatively empty, which allows them to slip through with a minor glamor. Hongjoong charms the ticket counter lady to get the number of the next bus that leaves St. Louis for Las Vegas. He moves on to charm the bus driver and convinces him they have valid tickets, and the cub is actually a service pup in training. Once Hongjoong gives Minseok the ok signal, he guides everyone into the bus and helps them situate themselves so he can look over all their injuries again as they wait.

They set Lauren up in the far back corner for protection reasons, and they all settle into seats around her and Hatawa.

It's a long day and a half trip. They take time to get food and eat at a few stops; they even find suitable food for Hatawa in his current form.

Still stuck in her emotions and fear of rejection from the coven, Lauren stays put and doesn't move unless she has to. At one point, she tries to give Hatawa to one of the other members, but he protests and clings to her, which confuses all of them enough that they don't fight his desire to stay with her. Seeing the others discuss his strange behavior makes her more concerned. When they aren't checking on Hatawa, they fall back into those pairs, but this time Tamryn sits beside her after another brief stop, still quiet as ever, and stays beside her for the rest of the trip.

By the time they reach the station in Las Vegas, they've all slept a proper amount and recharged. Minseok takes a minute to change Lauren's bandages and do a quick healing session on Hatawa just before they arrive, so they are fit to travel. Hongjoong explains they can teleport once they're out of the city, but the walk to the desert is long, so they all take precautions by shedding their winter coats before they begin.

Vegas is busy as ever, but unlike the cities of the east, it's full of strange groups of people, making it easy for them to blend into the crowds without magic. The heat is unbearable, though. The further north they walk, the less shade they find and the quieter the streets get. It's hours later that they reach the outskirts, where nothing but the desert stretches out before them to the horizon line. They're tired and exhausted, but they're finally safe from onlookers. After taking a minute to drink some water and breathe, they connect their hands once more. Hongjoong focuses on a place near his coven in his mind, and Nico channels the image to transport them to the location.

One second, they're in the scorching desert sun, and the next, they're under the shade of a tree. The heat of the sun still boils the air, but a fresh breeze brings them slight relief.

"Where are we exactly?" Nico asks as he studies the mountains and trees around them.

"Adaven," Hongjoong waves his hand for them to follow, "it's one of the few woodland places in this part of Nevada. Our coven established this location as a safe space from the other desert covens that used to rule the area."

"In the end, the High Coven put an end to them," Minseok adds.

"Yep. My mother built on the edge of our lands, seeing as she's a bit of an outsider, so her house should be - ah-ha!" They step out of the cluster of trees into a rocky area dotted with houses and witches. Before them sits a somewhat worn-looking wood building. In front of the house is a garden, full of plants used for potions, native to the dry landscape. In the garden stands a woman with silver-white hair tied in a messy bun. Hongjoong's face lights up, and he waves his arms. "Mom!"

The woman looks up in confusion. She scans the area; her eyes land on Hongjoong, then Minseok, and then the rest of the coven.

"Hongjoong, Minseok," she smiles and shakes her head, "what have you gotten yourselves into?"

Healing

With a big grin, Hongjoong runs to his mother. She catches him with ease as he wraps his arms around her. Minseok isn't far behind; he slings an arm around her shoulders in a gentle hug as he explains they need her help with an injured coven member.

"Oh, you have a coven!" she bounces on her heels. "I'm so happy for you two! Okay, let me see the injured one." She takes a second to look at the rest of them as they join the trio.

There's a tickle in the back of Lauren's head, like she's seen this woman somewhere, but she can't put her finger on where. Wrinkles and sunspots on her fair skin show her age. She only comes up to Hongjoong's chin and Minseok's shoulder and doesn't look to be too intimidating in stature, but the air around her is full of beauty and confidence.

Her eyes narrow in on Lauren and Hatawa. She takes in their state. "What have you been up to?"

"We'll explain it in more depth," Hongjoong pauses, then says, "but inside, out of earshot."

They shuffle their way into Hongjoong's family home, a modest and cozy place. The open floor plan makes it easy for everyone to settle in the living room. Hongjoong's mother, who introduces herself as Annabelle, takes Hatawa and places him on the dining table as Minseok explains what caused Hatawa's state, and Hongjoong fills her in on what they're up to.

"With Lauren's help, we're heading to the High Coven," Hongjoong finishes as he rubs his mother's back while she works.

"I told you it would happen someday. You just had to experience more before you could go to the High Coven. Both of you needed to get away." She smiles. "I'm happy you're still by each other's sides. Your mother," she turns to Minseok, "has been very worried about you."

"Ah," Minseok flushes, "I had a feeling she might be, but I had to go."

Lauren watches this interaction. With her mind no longer worried about Hatawa, she can once again study the dynamics of the coven. Here, she notes the looks that Minseok and Annabelle share.

"You two," she shakes her head and turns to Hatawa, "inseparable and perfect for each other."

A panicked look graces Minseok's face as Hongjoong laughs. "We are. I couldn't imagine my life without him. He's a very important person to me." He then gives Minseok a heart-stopping smile, which makes his face darken and relax.

Everyone is too busy enjoying the moment of peace and rest to notice Lauren back away and slip outside. She closes the door, rests her head on the wood, and listens to the laughter inside. She knows she should be with them. They've taken great care of her since the attack, but she still feels like she shouldn't be with them. As she shakes her head, she pushes off the door and walks over to a small well pump. Not concerned about the dust and dirt, she sits down. With careful movements, she removes the bandages on her arm. As the sun and heat touch the exposed skin, she winces, but she rinses them off and begins a healing session.

"There you are." The voice startles her out of her concentration. "Minseok thought you might heal your own wounds." It's Tamryn. He crouches in front of her.

"I can handle myself." The words come out of instinct. She almost regrets them, but Tamryn smiles and sits.

"We know," he pulls a roll of bandages from his pocket, "but help is always nice. Finish up, and I'll put these on for you."

She hesitates but starts healing again. They sit in silence. The sun sinks below the mountains as time passes. Tamryn summons a small glowing orb when the last rays disappear, casting enough light for Lauren to finish. Once he's sure she's done, he takes her hand and starts to wrap up her arm.

"Why?"

Tamryn hums and raises a brow.

"Why are you so nice to me? Better yet," she huffs, "why did you punch Damien?"

"Why wouldn't I punch him? He's an asshole," he states as she laughs, "but no one deserves to be treated like that, especially not you. You're innocent, and I know how it feels to be innocent and treated as if you aren't."

That surprises her. "What happened to you? If it's not too intrusive."

He barks out a laugh and smiles. "You are, at this point, a part of our coven in my eyes. Nothing is intrusive anymore." She tries to refute, but he moves forward with his story. "I was born to a coven in New Hampshire, one that tried their best to handle all their affairs without the High Coven's intervention. I wasn't well-liked; I was quiet and studied more than I socialized, but my sister and I were very close, and she loved how passionate I was about studying magic. The coven frowned upon it; they preferred fighting to studying. She would sneak around and find time to be with me while I studied. At some point, though, the stress of it all got to her, and she," he falters and pauses his movements, "well... she decided she didn't want to be here anymore. I was the one who found her." He sighs and ties off the first bandage. He grabs her other arm and continues, "And since I was the one who found her, they all assumed I did it. I don't remember their reasons anymore, but even my parents believed I did it. I think they were going to hang me, but I ran away. I took my sister's favorite book as a reminder and left. It wasn't until I met Joshua that I trusted a witch again. I still struggle with it. Even trusting the rest of the group we've created was hard. When your entire coven turns on you, it messes with your head." He ties off the last bandage and then takes her hand. "What I'm trying to say is I understand, and no one should be treated like that."

Lauren's cheeks heat up as he stares at her, his gaze warm and caring. Her stomach flutters as he raises her hand in his and places a gentle kiss on her knuckles. "I'm sorry that happened to you, but I'm glad you understand."

"I can't explain it, but I knew when I saw you that... I don't know." He runs his free hand through his hair.

"I get it," she smiles. "I mean, why else would you come to a random witch and comfort them when you have such trust issues." They laugh. "Knowing that, I guess it's just one of those instant connections."

He hums. "Poor timing, though. So much is going on right now."

"I know, but once it's all settled." She leaves the rest hanging between them. But he understands.

"Yeah," he squeezes her hand, "as soon as we get to the High Coven and things settle down. I promise," he lifts her hand and kisses it once more. "Let's go get some food, Minseok, and Hongjoong's mom are cooking. I think Joshua was going to help. He's been learning to cook."

When they return, still holding hands, no one comments, but a few give them looks, and Minseok makes sure Tamryn wrapped her wounds properly. Annabelle creates a space for everyone to sleep in the living area after dinner and sets up Hatawa in Hongjoong's old room, where Minseok leaves some of his clothes and a glass of water in the hopes he may shift back overnight.

In the morning, Minseok's mom comes over to see him and meet the coven. With

Minseok occupied, Lauren takes time to check on Hatawa between his healing sessions and sit with him while the others are busy. As she leaves his room later, she's pulled aside in the hallway by Rey.

"I found this by the riverbank before we teleported." He holds his hand out to reveal her mother's necklace.

"Oh my god!" She feels around her neck and then grabs it. "Thank you, you have no idea what this means to me, thank you."

"I thought it might be important," he points out, "you hold on to it when you're stressed."

She nods her head. "It's my mother's. I've been using it to track her, but tracking isn't my specialty."

"When was the last time she had this?"

"Right after I was born. Which is why it's so hard. Even if I had good tracking skills, it would be difficult."

He stares at it for a second, then tilts his head. As she turns to walk away, he reaches for her arm. "Wait. I could, if you want, see what I can get from it. Tracking is my specialty."

Her eyebrows shoot up. "That would be nice." She clears her throat and relaxes her features. "You don't have to, though. That would be helpful, and I'd appreciate it, but you don't have to."

"Don't be so scared," he laughs and rubs her head. "I think you may be a part of this coven yet. If you let me hold on to it, I can try finding some traces of your mother."

There's a genuine smile on his face that releases her tension. She places the necklace back in his hand. "Thank you. I'm aware I wasn't your favorite person when I shook up your coven's life, but I'm glad you don't hate me."

"Of course," he almost looks offended. "I mean, it was a rocky start, but I think we're finding our footing with you."

It's hours later when Hatawa makes progress. He shifts back, but it's a rough process. Hongjoong and Minseok coax him back and help him, but as soon as his form settles, he passes out from exhaustion; Annabelle gets to work on mending his wounds as they reopen. As the rest leave her to her work, Lauren watches from the doorway. She bites her thumb every time Hatawa's face twists in pain.

"You can join me," she says. "My son tells me he was protecting you?"

Lauren hums and sits on the bed beside Hatawa.

"Your attacker wasn't playing around." She pulls her hands and motions for Lauren to grab the bandages on the nightstand. "This is, by far, the most intense magic wound I've seen, and our coven members come in with some rather nasty ones. I'm always patching them up, it seems."

Lauren passes the bandages over and says, "My coven wants me dead. My father ha-" she hesitates, "he had information about them that would get them a full court trial and prison, if not death, and now I have the information."

"It's brave to be collecting any information like that on your own coven, especially one that's capable of this," she instructs Lauren to hold Hatawa up as she rolls the bandages around his chest. They work in silence for a few minutes, then they lay him back down. "If I may ask, how did you get the information? Did your father die?"

Lauren closes her eyes and nods her head.

"I'm sorry." She lays her hand on her shoulder with a gentle squeeze.

They share no more words. She finishes patching up his wounds and leaves to see about dinner. Lauren takes her chair and continues to sit with him. At some point, she closes her eyes and drifts off. She's surprised when she's woken by the gentle call of her name. After a couple of blinks, she finds the room has darkened, and there is a warm blanket around her shoulders. The voice calls her name again; she turns to see Tamryn next to her.

"Minseok wants you to eat," he explains.

She lets him pull the blanket off and help her up. They walk to the living room, where Hongjoong is asleep on Minseok's lap, and Rey and Nico are at the dinner table. In front of Rey sits Lauren's compass; it spins as he weaves his magic through it.

Tamryn sets her down next to him as she says, "You didn't have to mess with it now."

"Oh, but he did," Nico chimes in from his spot across the table, "he was going stir crazy. He's not able to track the High Coven, and it's driving him nuts. I swear if he didn't find something to do, I was going to strangle him."

Rey rolls his eyes. "You're so dramatic. I was just bored, and I've made headway! Your mother is close, like within the state close, I think."

"Really?" She perks up as Tamryn places a plate of food in front of her.

"Yeah, but I can't be totally sure, so don't get too excited. This will take a bit."

"Speaking of tracking, Hongjoong was wondering where the compass points to now," Tamryn sits by Nico and places the compass down. "Eat a little first, though."

After a few bites, she picks up the compass. Once again, she thinks of the High Coven and her desire to finish what her dad started. She pushes away the thoughts of her mother as best she can as the needle begins to spin. Just as fast as it started, it swings to an abrupt stop.

"Southwest."

"I'll recheck the maps," Minseok says as he rubs Hongjoong's shoulder, "after he wakes up."

"So whipped," Nico whispers to Rey, who giggles as Tamryn rolls his eyes.

As everyone settles down, a commotion comes from the other side of the house. All heads turn as a door opening follows a loud thud. Hongjoong wakes up as Azrael comes out from the hallway.

"Hatawa's awake!"

In the next instant, everyone is up and down the hall. They crowd into the room. Annabelle watches from beside the door as they surround Hatawa. Lauren trails behind and stays by the door as well as he looks around with a tired smile.

"Hey guys," his voice is hoarse; Minseok grabs the glass of water and holds it for him. After he takes a few sips, he asks, "Where's Lauren?"

All eyes turn to her. She twists her hands in her shirt and takes a breath before she walks up to the bed. Tamryn places a hand on her shoulder to ground her as she steps up to him.

Hatawa's smile grows wider. "I'm so glad you're okay."

"You?" she laughs, blinking back tears. "Hatawa, you scared me half to death. Why did you even do that? For me, of all witches?"

He gives a soft laugh, then clears his throat. "You don't know my powers, do you?" She shakes her head. "I'm a medium; it runs in my coven. We see and speak to the dead, if they're strong enough. Some spirits are faint, others are loud. I'll admit, I still wasn't keen on your magic loyalties when your coven showed up and chased us, but as I went back to find you, I heard you and Damien, and then I heard this ear-splitting scream of your name that didn't come from this plane of existence," he rubs his ear as if he can still hear it. "There was a spirit following you since we met, faint and barely there, but at that moment, they used all their strength left to form a barrier around you, and it was by far the brightest energy I've seen in a spirit. I only had a split second to react as Damien fired at you, but I knew that if a spirit with that much light in them was protecting you," he reaches to grab her hand, "then you have no true darkness in your own spirit. You've just been tainted, and that can be cleaned. I wasn't going to let you die like that."

Lauren doesn't realize she's crying until Tamryn rubs her back. Hatawa squeezes her hand once more.

"Sadly, their death damaged them," he continues. "It was a struggle for them to even manifest at all, so their presence before that moment and since then has been very faint, more so now."

A loud sob wracks through her body. She curls into herself as she tries to catch her breath. "My dad," she chokes out, "it was a train explosion that killed him. A train explosion started by pure hellfire. It was sudden and so destructive."

"That would be why his spirit isn't strong, but he has a very bright soul, and he's watching over you. When I'm stronger," he pauses and waits until she looks back at him, "we can do a séance, and you can speak to him."

Lauren nods, sniffling. "Thank you." She squeezes his hand and then pulls back to wipe her face.

Minseok makes Hatawa take another long drink of water and asks someone to get something for Lauren to drink. Annabelle is quick to offer herbal tea for everyone, and she ducks out of the room to give them time with Hatawa. He tries to get filled in on what he missed, but everyone insists he rests for the night. They stay with him for a few hours until they've finished the tea, and he's fast asleep. Azrael and Joshua remain in the room while the rest retreat to the living room for some much-needed sleep. At this point, the exhaustion settles in, and Lauren curls up against Tamryn, who holds her close as they sleep.

By afternoon the next day, they fill Hatawa in on the recent events and spread out the map over the table. Despite Annabelle and Minseok nagging at him to stay in bed, Hatawa is up. His strength isn't back, but he refuses to stay still any longer.

All of them sit and discuss the probable location of the High Coven. With most of them being from this side of the country, they know enough about which lands belong to covens and which ones don't. They rule out most major cities, being too populated for any kind of secrecy, and Hatawa pours his knowledge of the California mountain and valley covens onto the map. He reminds them he left California a long time ago, so the information may not be up to date.

"Alright," Hongjoong calls attention, "with everything we know, I think it's safe to say they aren't in the mountains, or anywhere between the mountains and the coast."

"That just leaves the Mojave, right?" Azrael leans over the map. "And if it's southwest of here, then you just have the empty Nevada desert and Death Valley."

Rey slumps back in his chair. "Both options are in an almost inhospitable land. Plenty of people live in the Nevada desert between the major highways, but Death Valley? Only a handful of people can live there year-round."

Minseok sits up and taps Death Valley on the map. "Then that's where they live, the one place no one would even think to search. Death Valley."

"He has an excellent point," Lauren says. "We can always test the compass as we get closer, but I think out of all the areas, that makes sense. No other covens have ever stayed there, right?"

"Right," Hatawa agrees, "my mom said every coven in this area has declared that spot too hostile."

Hongjoong clicks his tongue. "Okay, if everyone's on board with that, then we'll start there."

With confirmation from everyone, Hongjoong circles Death Valley and closes the map just as a knock comes from the front door.

"Stay," Annabelle sweeps into the room. "Hopefully, we aren't in trouble. Just stay there." They all share wary looks as she opens the door. She doesn't move for a second; she blinks up at the tall figure on the other side. "Richard, what are you doing here?"

"I heard your son had returned," a deep voice answers. A grizzly man with a clean-shaven head pushes his way inside, "With a bunch of witches that you are housing. Now you know we aren't keen on refugees and such, so I'm concerned about that." He stops as he looks at the rest of them. His eyes zero in on Lauren, and she shrinks back. "Why hello there, Lauren."

The color drains from her face. Everyone stands in defense.

"Kensington will be so happy you're safe and unharmed."

Annabelle snaps back into focus at this; she steps forward with furrowed brows. "Kensington?"

"Yes, her coven head." He waves a dismissive hand and gives Lauren a gut-churning smile. "He's been worried sick looking for her! Poor thing had a misunderstanding and ran off. By the way," he moves towards her, but Tamryn moves to block her. Richard gives him a bored look. "I am sorry for your loss. Your father was a good friend of Kensington's. Such a shame. I must inform him in the morning of your safety; they'd love you to come back to talk things over."

"I'm good," she says. "I think I'm fine without going back to my coven."

Unperturbed by this, Richard waves her off. "Either way, Kensington will be pleased.

I should get going. I just wanted to pop in and see," he flashes a smile. "They don't seem dangerous, so they can stay. Have a good night."

As quickly as he came, he's gone with a click of the door. No one moves or speaks; they take a second to process the new development.

Annabelle is the first to speak, voice soft as she turns to face them. "Kensington, as in Michael Kensington?"

Lauren pulls herself together. "Yeah, how do you know his full name?"

"I - wait, coven head?" she looks confused as she runs a hand through her hair and looks around the room. "He's coven head now?"

"Well, yes, and no?" she steps out from behind Tamryn. "He's been our High Priest since I was a kid."

"Oh, that's rich," she rolls her eyes, voice assertive now. "I leave, and he gets a promotion? I bet he gave himself that promotion too."

"Mom," Hongjoong tries to speak, but Lauren is already asking a question over him.

"You were in my coven?" she moves around the table. "My mom used to be in our coven as well. She left when I was born. Do you think you might have known her? Ah here, Rey, where's the necklace?"

Still shocked by everything, Rey takes a second to pull the necklace from his pocket and hand it to her. Once she has it, she walks across the living room to show her.

"This was her necklace," she holds it out so Annabelle can take it. "I found it in her old room before I left. I've been using it to track her. Rey said she may be close. Do you recognize it?"

Hongjoong moves to join them, muttering how his mom never talked about her past coven as he eyes Lauren. Annabelle looks down at the necklace. They wait as she turns it over and smiles.

"I do recognize this," she says. "This is my necklace."

Mother

"Mom," Hongjoong steps forward, "what do you mean?"

She looks at him, then to Lauren. "It's mine. My husband gave it to me for our -"

"Tenth anniversary," Lauren finishes.

Hongjoong turns to her and growls, "How do you know that?"

She flinches back. "It was the only piece of jewelry he ever gave her. Mom hated gifts, but their tenth year was special."

"Yes, he wanted it to be a moment to remember." With a fond smile, Annabelle looks down at the necklace. "I didn't think he'd have kept it after all this time."

"Mom…"

"I was going to tell you," she looks up at Hongjoong with watery eyes, "but I didn't think it would matter. I never in my life thought I'd see you again," she turns to Lauren, "and your father, I was sure I wouldn't ever hear from, so I just tried not to think about you."

"But he tried," Lauren cries, "he tried to find you! He has so much to explain; you need to know what happened!"

"No." She shakes her head and shoves the necklace into Lauren's hand. "No, we don't have time for that. I promise, both of you," she squeezes their shoulders, "I will explain, but right now, there's abou to be a hit squad on my doorstep."

"I'm sorry," the maps tumble out of Minseok's hands, "hit squad?"

"Yes. Everyone pack up." She leaves no room for argument as she takes off down the hallway.

Hongjoong and Lauren stare at each other. A new light shines in their eyes as they truly study at each other for the first time. Lauren can see a bit of her dad in some of his features, the way his mouth rests, the piercing look of his eyes; knowing what their mother looked like at one point and being told so many times that she looks like her, she knows he's seeing the same things her father saw.

"You guys heard my mom," Hongjoong turns to the coven, "let's pack up."

They gather their bags. Lauren grabs her satchel from the couch as Annabelle rushes back in. She brandishes a folder full of paper. "Take these," she says before she shoves it into Lauren's satchel.

Minseok asks. "What's that?"

"Proof. Medical papers of serious injuries, conversations I've overheard, and just," she waves her hands while walking to the door, "evidence against our coven. It's gone downhill since you two left, and since Richard took charge, he's gotten into some dark magic. This whole thing you've been studying since you were a teen, Hongjoong? Well," she pulls open the front door, a gust of wind sweeps inside. "Richard has made our coven the number two of this rebellion."

Hongjoong runs a hand through his hair, a trait of their father's, Lauren notes, as his other hand rests on his belt. "That's a lot to process. There's just... so much happening."

"Hongjoong, baby, this is a lot right now, I know," she walks to him and takes his face in her hands, "but I'll explain everything when I can. Right now, though, I need you all to get to safety. Please, just grab your things and follow me. I'll get you out, and you can get all this evidence to the High Coven. Okay?"

He nods his head and helps the rest finish packing.

They then step out into the gusty air and follow Annabelle back into the wild desert. The full moon above casts a blue hue over the dry landscape, giving enough light between the clouds for them to maneuver. The strong wind continues to kick up patches of dust and dirt that obscure their vision, but it's not long before they're breaching the tree line. They stand on the edge of the expansive and barren desert once again; the winds are stronger with nothing to block them. The only thing close to them is a small pile of stones that's been here for ages. Annabelle walks to this pile and holds out her hands as she begins an incantation. There's a spark in the air in front of the rocks; a portal tears open and swirls into shape before her. They see a new desert landscape through the slight purple hue of the magic, with snow-covered dirt and cactuses instead of sand. A few snowflakes flurry out from the portal, melting as the wind sweeps them away.

"This will take you to the other side of the Mojave near California." She looks to the portal and mutters, "I think."

"You think?" Nico raises a brow.

"I set it up ages ago, I can't be sure, but I have to close it on this side," she hesitates. "And it's one use. Once I close it, it's gone forever," she gestures to Hongjoong and Lauren, "your father taught it to me."

Rey walks to the portal and taps it while he asks, "And why do you have this?"

"For the girls, Hongjoong, and Minseok can explain more, but they are pretty much used as magic dispensers. I wanted us to have a way out in case -"

"In case what, Annabelle?"

The wind howls, another gust blinds them as dust swirls around and sweeps past them into the trees. Dozens of witches emerge from the tree line, each with a latched and loaded crossbow, and move to create a rough semi-circle around them and the portal. Richard looks at them with a smile as he repeats, "In case what, Annabelle?"

"Go!"

"I wouldn't do that," Richard says. "They're all fantastic shots."

As the witches step closer, they close ranks and push Hatawa to the back to keep him close to the portal for a quick escape. Hongjoong stands his ground and steps up front next to his mother.

"You can't stop us," he says, "one way or another, the High Coven is going to know of your crimes."

Richard rolls his eyes.

Annabelle turns and motions for them to head through the portal. Minseok nods in acknowledgment and starts by helping Hatawa step through, and then Joshua and Azrael as Hongjoong continues his speech.

"You should know by now; we will do what it takes to bring back order to the covens."

Richard shakes his head. "The old order has gone. The High Coven will realize this soon enough. Dark magic is true magic. Now look," he sighs, "I want the girl. Lauren has more information than anyone else. I can let the rest of you go with a slap on the wrist if you give her to me."

By this point, Rey, Nico and Tamryn are on the other side of the portal. Tamryn makes a move to come back through, but before he can put a single hand through, a snarl tears out of Hongjoong's throat.

"None of my coven is up for offer. They are not bargaining chips, and this is not a game."

"Hongjoong," Lauren steps forward to reach for him; a crossbow bolt punctuates her movement at her feet.

"That's a warning," Richard's face darkens.

Hongjoong looks back at Minseok. "Go."

He hesitates; worry is clear as he shifts from the portal to Hongjoong and back. Joshua pulls Tamryn back and reaches to take hold of Minseok's arm and helps him move through the portal to join them. As he goes, the remaining three move back to the portal with cautious steps.

Richard heaves a dramatic sigh. "Always the hard way," then he raises a fist in the air.

Every crossbow unlatches simultaneously, creating an echo around them that echoes through the trees. Despite the wind, the bolts fly true and fast. Lauren only has a split second to conjure a shield around them, deflecting most of the bolts. It cracks with each hit, and a few bolts make it past. They slice at their arms and legs as they try their best to stay covered.

"Reload and fire again!"

Annabelle spins around and takes each of their hands. "You have to go."

"Mom!" Hongjoong looks at her. "I'm not leaving -"

"You have to, and I have to close the portal from this side." She lets go of Hongjoong to run her hand through his hair.

"She's right," Minseok calls from the other side.

They hesitate, but as the crossbows latch, Hongjoong nods. Minseok reaches back through the portal and takes his hand before he can rethink anything. He squeezes his hand and takes Lauren's hand to pull her to his side as he places his foot through the portal.

"Aim for the redhead and fire!"

Mother

The crossbows echo once more. Lauren lets go of Hongjoong's hand to hold the shield steady as the bolts come towards her in a couple of staggered waves. The force of her letting go sends Hongjoong and Minseok tumbling into the dirt and snow on the other side. As he pushes himself up and turns around, the sound of the shield shattering penetrates the air like a gunshot.

Lauren stares in horror as shards of fading crystal magic fall before her, leaving her exposed as they fire another wave of bolts. She can't breathe or move, but in the next second, her view of the bolts and fading shield is thrown away as someone shoves her into the portal. Tamryn is quick to catch her, but she twists in his arms to see what's happening. It takes a second for her to register what she's looking at, but as blood spills from their mother's mouth, she knows what's happened.

"Mom!" scrambling his feet, Hongjoong makes a move for the portal.

Annabelle smiles, a few tears roll down her cheeks as she says, "I love you both so much."

The sound of the crossbow bolts is heard once more, and the portal closes right on Hongjoong's fingertips.

Silence.
No wind.
No movement.
No noise.
Hongjoong screams.

The Truth

Hongjoong's scream is like an open wound that's been stabbed into, gut-wrenching and filled with anguish. Lauren doesn't realize she's sobbing until Tamryn takes her in his arms and pushes her head into his shoulder. Her cries are as loud as Hongjoong's screams, which degrade into ugly sobs as Minseok wraps him in his arms and tries to calm him down as sparks burn the weeds at their feet.

In the end, Minseok and Tamryn get them both to sit down beside each other on a patch of dirt where Nico has cleared away the snow. Minseok directs the rest to keep watch and figure out where they are as Tamryn retrieves blankets from one of their bags.

"It's both for the cold and shock," he explains as he crouches down and drapes them over their shoulders. "It's winter. Moonrise is still yet to come, and it's the desert. It's going to be cold for you two."

"Thank you, Tamryn," Lauren manages a small smile as she pulls the blanket closed around herself.

Turning to Hongjoong, he says, "I know what you're going through. I'm sorry you have to experience this, both of you." With a glance at Lauren, he gives a tight smile. "We'll get through this together."

Hongjoong sniffles, rubs his face, and nods.

Hatawa looks around. "Judging by the lack of sand, I think we're close to California."

"Good," Hongjoong stands up. "We need to get to the High Coven, now."

Minseok places his hands on Hongjoong's shoulders and forces him to sit back down. "No, not like this."

"We have to!"

"NOT like this." He sighs, "Hongjoong, you are not in any condition to go out there. These witches are more than we were prepared for, and you are distraught."

"I'll be fine," he stresses the last word with a growl, which Minseok is quick to return.

"Rushing into Death Valley like this will only make us more vulnerable. We need to regroup, rest, and hide for a few days before we go charging into the fight again." He wipes the tears from Hongjoong's cheeks while trying to keep his own at bay. "You just suffered a tragedy; you lost your mother, and you aren't the only one hurting here."

"I'm fine" Lauren dismisses with a wave of her shaking hand. "I didn't, I didn't." She takes a deep breath. "I didn't know her as a mother, so it's fine," she chokes on the last word.

Everyone watches with bated breath as Hongjoong's face drops, a slow realization dawning.

Tamryn tries to speak. "Lauren -"

"I'm fine, Tamryn," heatedly she wipes away her tears, "why can't I stop crying?!"

As the wind picks up again, the light snowflakes swirl around them, and Hongjoong reaches over to take her hand. He pulls her close and wraps his arms around her while burying his head into her shoulder. He takes a few quick, shaky breaths. "We just lost our mom, and we lost our dad not even two months ago. But," he feels her cling to his back and pull him closer, "we found each other. Our coven is still here, and we have each other."

With a wet laugh, she gives a weak punch to his back. "I'm the older one here. Shouldn't this be reversed?" He laughs with her.

The rest of the coven watches with watery eyes. Minseok waves everyone over. They collapse into a tight group hug around the siblings, shielding them. After a while, Hatawa suggests they dig out their winter coats and put them back on before they make their way west into California. He suggests they seek refuge at his coven's home to rest and make a plan. Rey states that if he can find a landmark, he can orient them and guide them to Hatawa's home. Hongjoong doesn't fight as Minseok takes charge and gives them the green light for the plan. Given their emotional state, they keep Lauren and Hongjoong bundled up in the middle as they walk through the night. By sunrise, they find themselves on a paved road and follow it to a small town. With a location to go from, they pull out the map and make a route to Hatawa's coven. The stakes are high, so they all agree that teleportation would be too risky and continue on foot.

In the next major town, they stop for food and hunker down in an empty parking lot. Minseok takes a few minutes to check on each of them. He takes his time with Hatawa to make sure his strength is recovering. Once Minseok clears him, he takes his food and sits next to Hongjoong and Lauren, who are situated a few feet away from the rest.

Before they can ask him how he is or how he feels, he explains more about spirits. "When some people pass away, there's more often than not a part of them that stays here - that's what makes a spirit," he pauses to take a bite of his food. "Usually, they have someone to watch over, find, or protect. I spent most of my time after leaving home helping them - the spirits." By this point, he has their full attention. "I've held séances, helped them find their people, and guided them to the other side; it's what I excel at. Since we're going to my coven, I could do a séance. Bring your parents together so they can explain the things they didn't get to and so all of you can get a proper goodbye."

The siblings share wide-eyed looks as they contemplate the offer. Lauren smiles and nods.

Hongjoong gives his own nod and turns to Hatawa. "That would be amazing, but what about your strength?"

"By the time we reach my coven, I should be back up to par, don't worry." He waves him off. "I want to help you both get through this, and I think closure is the best way."

"Thank you, Hatawa." Lauren gives him a hug.

He wraps his arms around her and rocks her from side to side. "Anything for my family, which, by the way, Lauren," he pulls back, "welcome to the coven." He kisses her head and then takes his food and scurries back to the rest of the group.

With the smile still on her face, she watches the rest of the coven and asks, "Am I actually a part of this coven?"

"Of course," Hongjoong covers his mouth as he finishes chewing. "You're my sister, and aside from that, you've shown us how much you care. What you did for Hatawa; what you wanted to do for us. We may not have known you for long, but you are a part of this coven. I mean," he gives a sly grin as his eyes drift to Tamryn, "you and Tamryn seem to have grown very close."

Hongjoong laughs, and she sputters, "Yes? But no. I mean, it's ill-timed and less than ideal to start things yet, I'm sure you understand."

Hongjoong freezes. "How would I understand?"

She raises an eyebrow. "You and Minseok? You two seem to be holding off from becoming a thing as well."

Hongjoong's face in turn lights up a dusky pink as he starts to stutter and wave his hands. "What? No, no - we aren't - no, it's not like that."

"Oh, you don't realize."

"Realize what?" He motions her to be quiet as he looks over to where everyone is.

"You're in love with Minseok," the matter-of-fact way she says this makes Hongjoong recoil, "and he's so head over heels for you I won't be surprised if I find out one someone has a bet on how long it takes for you two to make it official."

Hongjoong stares at her with eyes wide and mouth open.

"Hongjoong," she giggles, "do you even realize you refer to Minseok as an 'important person?' Not coven member or friend or even best friend, he has his own title you use for him."

"Well, I mean." He closes his mouth and glances at Minseok. "I used to call him my best friend when we were younger, but after everything we've been through, it just didn't feel strong enough for our connection. He's my rock."

Lauren helps him along. "And why do you think that is?"

"Oh my god, I'm in love with Minseok," he groans, burying his head in his hands.

Lauren laughs and pats his shoulder. "You sure are, and, as I said, there's no doubt that he's in love with you, too. Probably has been for quite a long time."

"You also said now isn't the time." He lifts his head and bites his lip. "We've got a hard fight ahead of us, and there's no telling what'll happen when we reach Death Valley.

I don't think I should broach this topic; it may just complicate this whole situation. I shouldn't, should I?"

"That's your call," she shrugs. "I've only known you for a few months, but you need to let him know at some point. From what I can see, he seems content to just be by your side. He'd walk through fire for you." At that moment, Minseok looks at them. He sends Hongjoong a shy smile.

Lauren leans her head on his shoulder with a contented sigh.

Then Azrael shouts and jumps up. He points at Hongjoong and Lauren. Everyone stops; a rush of panic sweeps through them.

"I just realized something." He gives a sheepish smile and says, "when Hongjoong met Lauren, his powers didn't work on her. She's his biological sister! She's blood-related; that's why you couldn't mind warp her!"

Minseok agrees with a clap of his hands. "You're right! Hongjoong once tried to use his powers on his mom. They didn't work either. Got him grounded for a month, too."

"Yeah, dark magic has its limitations in strong familial bonds." Excitement rolls off

Azrael's shoulders. "Like, now that we are close to him even though we aren't blood-related, his powers have a diminished effect on us, but for blood relations, they can't be used."

Hongjoong groans. "That makes sense. I thought you might be some dark, powerful witch, but you're just my sister."

"That sounds like a bit of an insult." Hongjoong looks at her scowl, but it melts into a smile as she continues, "But I'm not super powerful, so I can't even be mad."

Everyone breaks out into laughter, which lightens the surrounding air. They continue to pick on Hongjoong as Joshua demands to know the story of him being grounded. Lauren listens as Minseok and Hongjoong tell the story. It's the first she has of her mother, and she hopes she and HOngjoong can continue to swap stories of their parents in the years to come.

The last leg of the trek doesn't feel as bad as the rest, and soon enough, they climb the mountainsides into the Stanislaus National Forest. Hatawa takes the lead as he begins to recognize certain trees and rock faces. The dirt and sand of the desert turn into slabs of rock and little lakes scattered between pine and maple trees. The higher up they travel, the colder it gets. Their breath turns into puffs of white air as they walk into snow and ice. Even though Hatawa swears they're close, Minseok makes everyone stop to bundle up before the cold gets to be too much. As soon as he's satisfied, they start again, and it isn't long before they reach their destination.

They reach the top of a cliff, and Hatawa breaks out in a run towards the edge and throws his arms out wide. "Home sweet home!"

Below is a small valley enclosed by sharp cliffs and thick patches of trees. In the center sits an open field dotted with buildings, farms, and the same small lakes they've seen throughout their hike up.

It's a peaceful sight.

"Come on." Hatawa waves to catch their attention as he walks down a narrow path on the cliff side. "This is the fastest way down. Watch your step!" He takes off without letting anyone ask questions.

"I think someone is happy to be home," Hongjoong laughs before ushering everyone to follow.

People in the village below take notice of the group; they must recognize Hatawa because there are some cheers as they wave to him. By the time they reach the bottom, a small group has swarmed Hatawa; all of them are asking questions and giving him hugs.

"I will explain everything later, but first, Mom," he takes the hands of an older witch who carries some of his strong features and pulls them forward. "I want you to meet my coven." He turns to face them with the brightest of smiles. He goes through them all one by one, stating their names and giving Hongjoong the title of 'leader of his coven.'

The woman, who has her pitch-black hair tied in a long braid, steps forward to shake Hongjoong's hand, "I'm so happy he found a coven. You all seem like such lovely people. All we ever wanted was for him to find his people."

Hongjoong gives her a hug. "You have an amazing son. He's become an integral part of this coven. We wouldn't be here without him."

With a gentle smack to Hongjoong's shoulder, she laughs. "Oh, stop it. You're definitely the charming one of the bunch." She turns back to Hatawa and asks, "Why are you home? This doesn't feel like a personal visit, and you all look dead on your feet."

They laugh and look away as if scolded by their own mother.

"We've gotten into a bit of a mess," Hatawa explains. "We need a place to lie low for a few days while we figure out our next move."

She hums and takes his hand, patting it. "Alright, come on, I think we've got an empty place with enough room for all of you to stretch out and relax. As we get you settled in, I'll send for your father, and you can explain everything."

After they settle into one of the empty houses - Hatawa's old hideout - they explain the whole situation to Hatawa's mother and father, a slightly taller and greyer version of Hatawa himself. He insists they contact a High Priestess to gain confirmation on their next steps. Hatawa's mother makes them agree to eat and rest an entire day before they do anything else. She cooks them a full meal. A few coven members come by to meet them and catch up with Hatawa; they learn that he's the star of his coven. He's very shy about it, which leads to the rest of them teasing him.

The jokes and laughter flow amidst the food and conversation.

When the moon rises, they all wind down and turn in for the night, except Lauren, who pulls Hatawa and Hongjoong aside.

"Would it be okay to do the séance tonight?" She asks.

Hongjoong rests a hand on her shoulder. "Tonight?"

She nods. "I think waiting for it is going to make it harder. I'd much rather just get it done with. I'm a little scared, honestly."

Hatawa and Hongjoong both soften at this. Hongjoong pulls her close and quietly agrees.

"We'll do it then," Hatawa says, "but I want Minseok and Tamryn with us. We have a few séance tables set up through the valley. The nearest one is a short walk away, but we can head out."

The night air is brisk. A thin layer of snow emits a coldness that seeps through their shoes as all five of them walk through the trees. Hatawa leads them along a well-trodden path. It turns into a long rock slab that slopes down into one of the many small lakes. At the end of the slab sits a round stone table, half in water and half on land, with a bench on each side. They all walk down to it as Hatawa explains, "Water is a great conductor for magic. Its movement and memory help spirits come to life and speak clearer by using its energy." He walks into the water, takes a seat on the bench, and motions for Hongjoong and Lauren to sit across from him. "Join hands and think of your parents. Lauren, think of your father and Hongjoong, think of your mother. I want to pull them both here, and it's easier if you both think of the ones you know most intimately. That way, the pull will be stronger."

They take a seat as Hatawa instructed. Tamryn and Minseok stand behind them, hesitant and nervous, but they don't want to interfere.

Once they make the circle, it's silent for a moment, then the water starts to move, lapping at the rock beneath them. Hatawa chants a little mantra under his breath as a breeze sweeps past; despite the winter air, it brings a warm and gentle feeling that soaks into their skin.

"Okay." Hatawa sits up straight and closes his eyes. "They're here."

Hongjoong sucks in a sharp breath; his eyes dart around. Lauren squeezes his hand.

"Annabelle Muldoon and Suho Kim," Hatawa smiles. "This is the first time they're seeing each other. I think your father is in disbelief."

Lauren takes a breath, eyes watering.

"They're happy though, shocked, but happy." His brows furrow. "They're blinking in and out a bit; he's trying to explain himself. Ugh, they're speeding up on me."

"Speeding up?" Minseok asks.

"When spirits feel intense emotions, they can switch to an ethereal time frame, which moves much faster than time in our world. Oh—wait, they're back," he dips his head in a nod and smiles. "Yes, hello! You're welcome."

Hongjoong smiles. "My mom is thanking you, isn't she?"

"She is," Hatawa opens his eyes, "and she wants you to know that she chose to save us. She doesn't want you to feel guilty about what happened." Hongjoong takes a deep breath and puffs out his cheeks, trying to relax. "She wishes she could've stayed, but she's still happy. Lauren, she says she's happy she got to meet you at least once, and," he closes his eyes for a second. "Your father says he's sorry. He realizes now that you were right, and he shouldn't have dismissed you as he did; he's proud of you."

Lauren breaks, she hangs her head, and shrinks into herself, but keeps the circle sealed; Hongjoong tosses his head back to blink away his own tears.

"They are both happy that you found each other; they can't imagine what would happen if either of you were left alone. Your mom says she wants to explain everything, so let me allow her to speak." Hatawa relaxes his body. He sinks forward as he closes his eyes. The water around him pulses from his feet as a glow takes over his body. With his eyes still closed, he sits up, and their mother's voice echoes out beside his. "I had planned to return to you, Lauren. I was hurt and emotional, but I had always planned to return. Then I got sick. I hadn't even realized how far I'd gone until the coven found me. It was there I found out I was pregnant, and I knew it would kill the baby and me if we traveled all the way back. It had been so long since I'd left, I thought it best to just stay and raise him there. I wanted to go back, but the longer I waited, the harder it was. In the end, I got tangled up in the mess you saw, and there was no way to leave. I wish you two could have met under better terms, but I'm so happy did."

"Did dad tell you what happened?" Lauren blurts out, hand crushing Hongjoong's.

Another warm breeze sweeps past them with the soft scent of a smile.

"He did, so I know what happened. Thank you, Lauren, for always looking for me. Your father would like to speak now, hold on." The glow fades for a second before a new, duller one takes over, and their father's voice comes through. "Hongjoong, my son," the voice wavers and cracks. "I'm heartbroken that I'll never be able to meet you physically. I've dreamed of having a son since Lauren was born, and I couldn't ask for a better one. I've been watching you, and I understand every choice you've made since you met Lauren. I know you'll protect your coven well. I am so proud of you both. Even if your mother and I aren't with you after today, we'll be waiting for you both on the other side." His voice fades away as Hatawa's body goes slack, his grip loosening as his body slips backward. Tamryn and Minseok jump forward to catch him. They sit him up straight as he blinks away the fog.

Lauren breaks into sobs, body shaking while Hongjoong has long, silent, tear tracks on his face. While Lauren curls in on herself, Hongjoong wraps her in his arms and holds her. He wants to tell her it's okay, but he knows it would be a lie.

Hatawa gathers his bearings. The toll of his magic is evident. "I'm glad I could give you guys this bit of closure. They haven't gone yet; I think they're going to be with you for a while longer before they're ready to pass on."

Under the moonlight, they rest until all the heavy emotions have passed. Hongjoong hands Lauren off to Tamryn and then leans into Minseok as they begin the hike back. Minseok and Hongjoong head off to their room; as soon as they step inside, Hatawa heads over to check in on his parents, which leaves Tamryn and Lauren.

"They set me up with a room for myself," Lauren says as they walk down one hall. She stops at the door and turns to him. "Could you stay, though? I don't think I can be alone right now, and I know we're still new to each other, but -"

Tamryn cuts her off. "I'll stay."

They hold eye contact for a minute. He takes her hand and gives her a reassuring nod as they head into the room. As soon as the door closes, Lauren collapses. Her knees give out, and tears pool in her eyes. Tamryn quickly catches her and pulls her up into his arms; he walks them over to the bed. He takes a minute to coax her to take off her shoes and coat, then he helps her lie down and sets aside his own shoes and coat.

Lauren grabs onto him as soon as he joins her, curling into him as she tries to muffle her cries in his shirt.

Tamryn's heart breaks. He holds her as close as he can, running a hand through her hair to calm her down. He lays a gentle kiss on her head, whispering, "You are so strong. I know this is hard, but you'll be okay. We're all here for you now. We won't leave you behind."

On the other side of the house, Hongjoong is in a similar state to Lauren. He walks into his and Minseok's room and sits on the bed, frozen. His brain races through everything that's transpired. Minseok watches from across the room, piercing eyes taking in every slight twitch Hongjoong makes. He wants to ask if he's okay, but it would be a stupid question.

Finally, Hongjoong breaks the silence and says, "I think for the first time in my life I'm actually scared. I have no idea what is going to happen to any of us. I never thought death was something I would have to come face to face with, which seems stupid now, but I just," his eyes don't move, glazing over. "I just don't know what to expect. I can't control what happens next."

"It's okay to be scared." Minseok walks over and sits next to him. "No matter what, though, I need you to understand that we're doing the right thing."

Hongjoong gives a dry laugh as he looks down. "I know." His hands twist together. "There's something I need to tell you, but I want to wait until this all levels out."

"Okay." He draws the word out with hesitation.

"It's not bad!" He looks at Minseok, eyes wide and innocent. "I promise, it's not bad, it's just... a lot. Everything is a lot right now. I just need to breathe for a day or two before we charge into the fight."

With a smile, Minseok lays a hand over his. "It's okay; I understand. You need to sleep."

"I know," he looks back down, "let's go to bed before it gets any later. We can rest tomorrow and call the High Priestess the next day. From there we can-"

"Stop." Minseok places a hand over his mouth. "Turn off your leader brain. We'll handle it as a coven later. Right now, let's go to bed."

Hongjoong does his best not to think about Minseok's hand or how close they are. He concedes with a nod and allows Minseok to pull him up to get ready. As soon as they're settled, and his head hits the pillow, Hongjoong falls asleep.

Next Steps

As the sun rises, the coven does as they promised, and takes the day to recharge and rest, starting by sleeping in for the first time in what feels like years. They forgo breakfast for a large brunch once everyone wakes up. Minseok does a preliminary check on each of them while they eat, allowing him to collect levels to base their following results on. While some protest that he needs to rest as well, he declares that this is his form of relaxing and refuses to let go of his tablet at any point. Hongjoong and Lauren negotiate with the coven to have a few hours of work amid their relaxation since the evidence their mom gave them needs to be gone through. They are able to get the coven to give them three hours to work by agreeing to take a break halfway through.

The pair separates the evidence from both their parents based on the coven it pertains to. Some of their father's information crosses over into Hongjoong's coven while some of their mother's information crosses over into Lauren's. They agree that depending on what they learn from the High Priestess, they will only take what they need for the final trip, and each will carry their own evidence. Hongjoong keeps the information about his coven, and Lauren keeps the information on her coven; she puts her evidence into her satchel once more while Hongjoong takes a pack from Minseok to store his evidence in.

Once they are done, the coven drags them in different directions for more relaxing activities that keep them busy.

When the sun rises the following day, Hongjoong gathers everyone into the small living room, and Minseok does his next evaluation of everyone's energy levels.

After he finishes, Hongjoong stands up. "It's time to call the High Priestess. We need to finish this."

"I say we contact Tamara specifically," Rey says. "She's helped most of us before, and I think she would be more willing to divulge their location than others."

"That's true," Azrael agrees. "She knows us already, but can you ask for a specific High Priestess?"

Minseok sighs as he brushes his hair back. "Maybe? With Hongjoong's magic, we may be able to focus on her and project our thoughts to her alone. We know her name, what she looks like, and her voice; if we all concentrate on that, we could summon her here."

Lauren raises a hand and asks, "What about protection? The last time we saw the High Priestess, we ended up in the crosshairs of my coven. They can track astral projections in the area."

"Hopefully, they don't know where we are, and even if they do, my coven has state-of-the-art protection runes set up throughout the valley," Hatawa says to reassure her.

Satisfied, Lauren relaxes back in her seat.

"We've only got one shot at this," Hongjoong continues. "We summon her, ask for confirmation and advice, and then we prepare. I have no idea what is going to be waiting for us, but as Minseok keeps reminding me," they share shy smiles as Minseok rubs his shoulder, "we are doing the right thing. Getting to the high coven and giving our testimonials will save other covens. We have to do this."

"We're here to the end, Hongjoong. This is our coven," Nico reassures, getting a round of agreement from everyone in the.

"Alright. Let's do this."

Minseok re-describes Tamara for everyone to make sure her image is fresh in everyone's mind before joining hands. It's an old-school summoning method; it won't bring them here, but rather, it forces the summoned person to astral project. They all take a second to focus on the image of Tamara as Hongjoong calls out to her both aloud and in his mind. There's a tug. Everyone's energy is pulled towards Hongjoong. It's silent for a few long minutes as they wait, and then in a flash of hot white light, Tamara's astral form appears in the middle of their circle.

"Did you contact me directly?" Her voice is airy and sharp. There's a hint of anger in her brows as she stares Hongjoong down. "On a direct line, really?"

"We needed to speak with you, just you." Hongjoong let his hands fall, not needing the circle of energy anymore. "We need you to answer a few questions."

Tamara tilts her head. "You are aware that we are not allowed to divulge private High Coven information to anyone, especially stray witches, correct?"

Nico scoffs, rolling his eyes as he mutters, "Still not a coven in their eyes, I see."

To which she turns to glare at him. "You're all stray witches until your coven is in the book. I was nice before, but this," she makes a gesture with her arms, "is pushing my patience. No one has ever forced a High Coven Priestess to make a showing. I am not happy."

"Then we'll make this quick; like I said, we only have a few questions. We won't ask the exact location, we have the compass for that, but we need to know if you are in Death Valley."

She eyes him for a minute, then says, "Yes."

Everyone lets out a sigh of relief.

"Perfect," Hongjoong claps his hands. "We can find you with the compass from there. Death Valley is expansive. It's not like we can just pop in. My second question is much more important; that's regarding what we are up against. While we were at mine and Minseok's coven, we were met with a much more brutal set of witches than we expected." He pauses, eyes hazy for a second, before he shakes his head. "Lauren's coven even turned out to be more violent and deadly than expected. This resistance we're up against, are they more bloodthirsty than we expected, and will we run into them on our way to you?"

Tamara tenses and crosses her arms with a heavy sigh. "The resistance has gained quite a few witches in its top ranks that will kill on site instead of capture. We have now lost contact with your coven, so I can only assume the worst," she muses. "Now, I am not supposed to tell you anything - being stray witches and all - but there is a concern we have been having. A coven of coyote shifters surrounds the valley we live in. This coven knows how to fight in the desert; they have killed quite a few of our scouts, they will not let you through without a fight. I am sure they are expecting you as much as we are. You will need to be at your peak energy levels and rested for the fight because there will be a fight. I wish I could say that you can just stroll on in, but it will not be that easy. I am hoping you make it, but they are ruthless."

In another burst of light, Tamara vanishes, leaving behind a thick layer of suffocating tension. They all look at one another with ranging levels of shock and concern.

"No matter what," Hongjoong says, "like Nico said, this is our coven. No matter what we face or what happens, this is our coven, and we fight for our coven."

Over the next few days, they prepare. With the knowledge of what they'll be walking into, it becomes apparent to them they will have no choice but to use weapons. They explain to Lauren that they try to stick to non-lethal magic, but they've kept their weapons close in case of emergencies.

Given the little time they have, they work to re-familiarize themselves with each of their personal weapons. One by one, they pull out their weapons and spread them out to assess, clean, and prep them. Lauren hasn't used weapons before, so she sits on the couch and watches them while asking the occasional question. Her first question is directed at Rey, who has a specialized bow.

"Why not a crossbow?" She asks him as he polishes the wood.

Rey says, "Way too long of a reload. Getting the bolts to latch can take a few seconds longer than notching an arrow, and those few seconds are important."

"Hey," Nico reaches out and rubs his arm. "Is that still bothering you?"

"Of course! You almost died," he stresses the last word as he places his hand on. "I almost didn't reload in time, and you almost died."

Nico smiles and shifts closer to try to relax him. "But I didn't, and you saved me."

Tamryn drops onto the couch next to Lauren, a cloth full of throwing knives in his hands. Rey and Nico slip into their own world, so Tamryn takes it upon himself to explain for them as Nico continues to calm Rey. "Their coven is the very definition of homophobic, and many of their fellow witches tried on many occasions to make them rethink their sexuality. They took it way too far in the end and tried to kill them."

Lauren's jaw drops. "What?"

He hums as he picks up his bag of knives, cleaning and polish them. "That was the event that led to Rey asking for guidance from the High Priestess, who ended up being Tamara. That led them to run away. Rey was back and forth between a crossbow and a traditional bow, but after almost not saving Nico with the crossbow, he chose the bow."

Lauren lets out a breath and looks back at the couple. "That's just insane. I'm glad they're here, though."

"So am I." Tamryn reaches out and squeezes her hand.

Nico joins Tamryn in cleaning their arsenal of knives. They explain that when Tamryn first joined, it was what they bonded over, and they now have quite the knife collection between the two of them. Joshua shows off his staff, pointing out the spells carved into the center where he holds it. Some spells are simple protection charms, while others allow him to use elemental magic like Nico.

"See, I don't need any of these fancy weapons." Hatawa boasts as he strolls past them. "I just need to shift, and I am a weapon! Ow!" He winces as Joshua smacks him on the back of the head.

The last weapon in their arsenal is a pair of gauntlets Azrael uses to channel his magic, which Hongjoong and Minseok helped him fashion with claws for protection way back when they all first met. Hongjoong and Minseok stick with their natural claws; they learned to shift just their claws to use when in scuffles with their coven.

Lauren explains to them she doesn't have any real fighting experience outside of what they've been through. "I've used my magic, of course," she says, "vines mainly, but if we're going to a desert, I don't know how useful that will be. I had a few lessons with knives in early schooling, but I declined most other weapon courses."

"We can teach you a few tricks," Hongjoong reassures her. "We're not going into this unprepared."

They spend some extra time teaching her a few of their fighting techniques. Nico takes it upon himself to help her get a feel for knives and helps her learn to throw and slash with precision. They all take a little time to show her something, making sure she knows enough to fight and defend.

This continues for a couple more days: rest, practice, plan, and repeat. Hatawa's family helps Nico find a safe area for them to teleport to in Death Valley. He familiarizes himself with pictures and their memories of the few times they visited. They make a general plan based on their destination and finish packing the few essentials they need for the fight.

Then it's time to say goodbye.

Blood-Soaked Sand

To prepare for the harsh weather of Death Valley, they all dress in pants and coats to cover as much skin as possible. Hatawa's father helps them gather the proper boots that are durable enough for the rocky landscape. Lauren ties her hair up in a tight bun to prevent it from getting in the way and then ties a knife belt around her waist alongside Tamryn and Nico. Rey situates his quiver strap and does a couple of test reaches to make sure it's easy to access. Azrael stashes his gauntlets in the pockets of his long coat, and Joshua simply carries his staff with him. Hongjoong lets Minseok add a few extra things to his pack before strapping it on; Lauren takes her satchel and secures it like she always does.

Everything else they leave behind.

They bid a solemn farewell to Hatawa's family. Hatawa promises everyone that they'll be back as soon as they can, but none of them make any promises to stay safe, and Hatawa's coven doesn't give them any real well wishes. They all know what they're walking into, and the possible outcomes aren't good. When the silence becomes too much, Hatawa pulls his parents into a death grip hug; his parents hold on to him for a few minutes before they force him to let go. His eyes are wet, but he takes a deep breath and steps away.

With the coven watching, they walk to the edge of one of the lakes, join hands, and close their eyes.

The cool mountain air is replaced by hot rays of sun and an expanse of dry, cracked desert. Harsh winds buffet into them. It takes them a second to get their feet steady in the flowing sand, but once they do, they take stock of where they are and check around for any buildings, landmarks, or hints of civilization. Upon finding none, Lauren takes out the compass. The needle swings and points behind them to their left. They turn and stare at a fast-growing sandstorm a few miles ahead.

"That can't be good," Nico comments with a frown.

Hongjoong says, "It's probably the coyote coven they warned us about."

"Alright everyone, take one." Minseok reaches into Hongjoong's pack and pulls out a small bag. "These charms will keep our body temperatures down so we can stay bundled up without dying of heat exhaustion." He opens it and rattles the charms around before holding them out for everyone to take one. They each put the charms in their pockets and make sure they can't fall out or get lost.

"Lauren, Nico, take the lead," Hongjoong orders. He motions for them to start the journey. "Stay close. Stay sharp."

The cloud of dust and dirt encases them slowly. Nico uses enough magic to push the storm away and give them a small sphere of dimly visible landscape. They close in ranks the further they go, the sun barely able to breach the walls. Lauren makes sure the compass's needle stays north even though she stumbles every once in a while with a good gust of wind; she keeps pressing on. They stop every few paces to let Nico push the storm back and give them room to move without being pelted by stray pebbles and rocks.

"At the pace we're going," Hatawa raises his voice above the howl, "I don't think we've made it very far."

"Yeah, well," Nico pushes the wall of dust a little further back as it closes in on them, "this is some powerful magic we're working against."

Azrael adds, "Not demonic, thankfully."

"I bet if I try to fly up, I still wouldn't see anything." Tamryn sighs.

With the dirt and sand digging into their hair and skin, they itch to reach their destination. Lauren tries her best to pick up the pace. The pattern of stop and go continues for a while longer until something appears in front of them. Nico drops his hands; he stares down at the large dark shape inside the storm. Azrael and Hatawa move to stand beside him as he pushes the storm away with each step they take. Lauren hangs back, squinting to try to discern the shape. It splits into multiple shapes as the dust begins to clear, then reveals itself to be a group of coyotes, sitting, waiting. Their ears twitch, eyes unblinking. Nico drops his arms, sweat dripping down his temple. The storm stays, which gives them an unobstructed view of the coyotes as more walk out of the wall behind them. They walk around and form a circle, caging the coven in and causing them to take defensive stances while drawing their weapons.

Despite the howling wind, a single bird cries out. A vulture cuts through the wall; it swoops past and causes them to duck down to avoid its wingspan. Its eyes seem to shine as it swings around and morphs into a person as it lands behind the coyotes.

Lauren's heart stops, limbs locking in place.

"Kensington."

Her old coven leader smiles. "It's nice to see you again. You've caused quite a ruckus." He looks over the rest of the coven. "All of you have made a rather useless mess." Before he can speak another word, a single knife flies through the air. He flicks it away and watches it vanish into the storm.

"You're done talking," Nico says as he reaches into his belt to grab another.

Hongjoong takes Lauren's hand and pulls her back to look at the compass. "The

High Coven is somewhere ahead of us; we have to be close."

"Close, but not close enough," Kensington mocks.

This time, Rey notches an arrow and fires to shut him up, which agitates the surrounding coyotes, but they hold their line.

"I can go," Tamryn steps up. "I might not be adapted to deserts, but I can fly through the storm."

Something tugs at Lauren's heart. It tells her to say no, but she agrees. As Rey fires another arrow, this time at the coyote next to Kensington, Tamryn shifts. His white feathers don't blend in amid the brown and beige tones, but he moves fast and launches himself up above them as Nico throws knives at the coyotes to distract and push them back.

It only lasts a few seconds.

Kensington snaps his fingers, and just as Tamryn flies over him, a different coyote emerges from the dust, with its jaw open, straight for the owl.

"Tamryn!"

Bones crunch.

Blood-Soaked Sand

The coyote's jaw snaps around his
middle. Blood sprays, the wind scattering it
as the coyote lands and tosses him. His owl
body tumbles across the sand, morphing
back into his pale, human face; he gasps for
breath as blood gushes from his chest.
Minseok and Lauren rush to his side.
Minseok rips off his coat to cover the wounds
and apply pressure, while Lauren begins
healing as much as she can.

With tears in his eyes, Minseok presses
down, which causes Tamryn to scream. "You
know you aren't supposed to shift back with
a serious injury! You bleed out faster!"

As her hands shake, Lauren stares in
horror. The magic proves futile given the
extent of the wounds. "Minseok, I don't
think—it's not working!"

"From what I have been told,"
Kensington calls out, "you will need a High
Priestess to heal those wounds. It is their
specialty," he reaches down to pat the head
of the coyote, blood coating its muzzle as it
seems to smile.

Hongjoong sees red. A ball of hellfire
forms in his hands. He steps forward and
throws it. The coyotes scatter, yipping and

barking as they run back into the dust, which sweeps the flames away in a heavy gust. Kensington wipes the flames off himself, face blank as he brushes off his sleeves.

"Temper tantrums will get you nowhere," he says.

"I'm going to kill you." Hongjoong snarls, each word pushed through gritted teeth as he conjures another ball of fire.

Behind him, Minseok works to slow the flow of Tamryn's blood in Lauren continues healing as much of the wound as she can, even trying to shift the blood to stay in him. More blood slips past his lips as he coughs, eyes squeezed shut.

"Hongjoong!"

He looks at Minseok's tear-streaked face.

"We need," he takes a shaky breath. "We need to take him to the High Coven. We need a plan." He presses down again on the wound as he turns to keep his eye on him.

Hongjoong hesitates. He glares at Kensington and the coyotes reemerging, then drops the fire and turns to the coven. "I may be the fastest shifter, but I know I can't carry Tamryn, so who's our next fastest?"

"Me." Nico steps forward and stows his knives.

"Put Tamryn on his back, give him the compass, and we'll get you through," Hongjoong orders. "Get Tamryn to them, get reinforcements, and get back." He conjures a fireball once more and throws it at the coyotes again.

Kensington grins and says, "If you think I am going to let any of you leave, you are sadly mistaken."

Minseok works to wrap Tamryn's wound with the coat as Nico passes Lauren his knives and shifts into a brilliant black and white husky. He crouches down so they can lift Tamryn onto his back; Tamryn screams again from the movement. They situate him securely on Nico's back as one coyote throws its head back to release a high-pitched howl. The others respond with yips and howls, and then they descend.

"They need to go, right now." Minseok tightens the coat around Tamryn as Lauren places the compass in Nico's mouth.

As the coyotes charge, Hongjoong channels his magic to create a spinning disk of black energy above his head. "Everybody down!" They move closer to Nico and drop to their knees as Hongjoong's magic pulses out, sending a shock wave of demonic black mist. It throws the coyotes back and breaks apart the sandstorm to reveal a frightening number of coyotes waiting in the distance.

"Oh shit," Azrael mutters as the storm rolls back in, closing around them again.

"Nico, go!"

Not wasting another second, Nico pushes off the sand, teleporting a few feet at a time in the direction they were first headed. The storm closes around him before the coyotes can get their bearings to follow; there's a moment of relief that sweeps through them, but then the coyotes howl. It echoes through the storm. Their eyes turn red, black mist lifts off their fur as they stalk towards them.

"Um, guys." Rey notches an arrow with shaky hands and looks around. "I don't think these are shifters."

They close ranks, forming a circle around them once more.

"Hell hounds," Azrael says under his breath. "They're just coyotes turned into Hell Hounds."

"Is that even legal?" Lauren draws two knives.

Hongjoong steps back and conjures another fireball. "Oh, definitely, and it's something the High Coven would know about."

With a tight grip on his staff Joshua says, "So either they don't know, or Tamara purposefully lied to us."

Their deliberation is cut short by another high-pitched yowl, signaling for the hell hound coyotes to descend on their prey. Kensington grins as he sinks into the storm, disappearing before Hongjoong can throw the fireball at him. He instead hurls it in Kensington's general direction and watches it disappear into the dust and sand.

As the wind swirls around them, they're charged from every angle. Azrael turns and grabs one coyote by its muzzle, throwing it aside while he lands a punch to the flank of another that lunges for Rey, who fires as many arrows as he can. He aims for heads and shoulders to slow them down. Hatawa shifts into a large black bear and charges right into a cluster of them, batting some aside with a few easy paw swipes.

"They don't seem as strong as Hell Hounds should be," Lauren says as she sidesteps one and throws a knife into its side.

"They aren't full Hell Hounds yet," Azrael calls out. He takes the leg of one and tosses it towards Hatawa, who sinks his claws into its side as it lands at his feet. "They're getting stronger with each passing second, though, so don't expect them to stay–" he's cut off by a coyote slashing at his leg. He kicks it aside and stumbles back into Joshua. Using his staff, Joshua sweeps the sand into the approaching coyote's face before setting Azrael back on his feet to land the next blow.

Hongjoong and Minseok fight back-to-back against a handful of them, going for their underbellies and flanks. Quite a few retreat into the storm, blood dripping from their bodies, but more emerge, fur smoking as they snarl and bark.

"We're going to get tired out before we make a dent in their ranks," Minseok points out as he tries to slow his breathing and dodge another coyote's bite. Lauren throws a knife at the coyote, pulling another out of the one at her feet before moving away.

"Jump!" Joshua swings his staff, sweeping it across the ground, sending a flurry of sparks and flames, which Lauren jumps over as the rest of the coyotes run away. Rey picks a couple of them off as they scurry away.

The next round of coyotes are bigger, smoking almost entirely as they rush them. Azrael only has a second to prepare before one has his leg in a death grip. The bone snaps under the pressure. Despite the excruciating pain, he punches it in the head and shakes it off before he falls to the ground. Minseok rounds on the coyote, slashing at its stomach before it can roll back over. Joshua steps in, knocking another out of the air before it can reach them while Minseok drops to Azrael's side.

"I know it's broken." Azrael waves him off through gritted teeth.

With a roll of his eyes, Minseok starts a healing spell. "Yeah, I gathered that; just let me patch it up a bit."

"Joshua!"

Lauren throws a knife, distracting the coyote that's approaching him. It turns its red eyes to her and charges, kicking off the ground with a cloud of sand. She steps backward a few times as she reaches for a new knife and slips. Falling, she realizes she's out of them. Casting the first spell in her head, she throws the coyote to the side, knocking into Hatawa. Hongjoong tries to aid them, but another group cuts him off from Hatawa as he rears on his hind legs.

"Joshua, help Lauren," Minseok orders, using part of Azrael's coat to cover the wound, "and you don't move." He creates a glamor barrier around Azrael, shielding him from the storm and coyotes.

As Lauren gets to her feet with Joshua's help, Rey takes care of the surrounding coyotes, and once they're on their feet, he goes back to the ones around Hatawa. Minseok returns to Hongjoong's side, fighting with him as another group of coyotes charge.

"Don't they ever stop?" Joshua screams, swinging his staff into another.

By this point, the heat, the wind, and the fighting have them drained. Dust and dirt mark their skin and clothes, speckled with blood from scratches and bites; no matter how hard they fight, they're still losing.

"I really hope Nico can get us help," Lauren breathes to Rey, "quickly."

A sudden wave of heat bursts from the wall of dust; Joshua tries to block whatever is coming out, but he's thrown off his feet and sent sailing. Hatawa stumbles, shifting back to his human form to curl into a ball and roll away. With no one to catch him, Joshua slams into the ground, head-snapping against the rough terrain. His staff slips from his fingers, and his eyes roll back, body going limp. Before any of them can check on him, the sound of shattering glass reverberates in the open air, followed by Azrael's scream of agony. Above him, with one foot pressing down on his broken leg, is Kensington, looking unbothered and bored.

"I was getting tired of waiting for you to die," he says. "I'll admit you've held your own pretty well, but I think it's time we end this."

Hongjoong immediately sends a black ball of fire at him, which he waves away, sending it careening towards Rey and Lauren. Wrapping an arm around Lauren's waist, Rey throws them both to the side. They land with a heavy thud as the fire flies past. Rey launches back onto his feet; he notches an arrow and fires at Kensington. He doesn't even flinch as he steps off Azrael's leg to swat each arrow away, but Rey doesn't stop until he reaches back to find his quiver empty.

"Alright," Kensington claps his hands, approaching Rey. "That's enough." He sweeps his hands out in a quick gesture that sends a bolt of flames directly for Rey's face. He only has a split second to turn, then the flames tear across the left side of his face, burning, his skin instantly boiling at a hellfire temperature. The scent of burnt flesh hit's Lauren's nose as Rey falls next to her, screaming in absolute horror as the searing pain takes his entire focus. Lauren crawls to his side, trying her best to hold him still enough to heal the still burning flesh.

A sudden scream comes from behind them, like a battle cry as Nico comes flying

out of the storm, eyes wide with a crazy
glint as he charges Kensington, drawing a
knife and slashing away. Kensington side
steps each attack, a smug smirk plastered
on his lips as he dances around Nico.
Hatawa rushes to help, only to be blindsided
by a couple of coyotes that take him to the
ground. Kensington spins behind Nico, and
he sees Hatawa, which causes his rage-filled
haze to fade for a moment, and Kensington
takes it. His hands morph into talons, and
just as Nico focuses back in on him, he
brings his hand down across the right side of
his face, tearing through his skin, sending
blood splattering across the ground. This
doesn't deter him in the slightest, though.
Blood drips from his eye socket, and his
vision grows hazy as more blood covers his
face, pouring from the wounds, but he spins
around and sinks his knife into Kensington's
chest. He goes to draw the knife out when a
coyote charges him, so he dives to the side
and falls into the sand near Joshua's
unconscious body.

With a groan, Kensington pulls the knife
from his chest. The blood on the blade
glistens an unnerving shade of black red in a

stray ray of sunlight. The surrounding storm seems to glitch, jerking into a slow swirl before picking up speed again. Sunlight breaks through cracks forming in the wall. He wipes the blade off on his arm and twirls it around as he faces the group once more.

"Looks like the High Coven has arrived." He points the knife at Lauren. "No more games; kill the two with the packs and shred the evidence."

Lauren's head jerks up, hands still hovering over Rey's face as several coyotes turn to her. The storm starts clearing, exposing more, all with their red eyes targeted on her and Hongjoong, who stands across the battlefield by Minseok. Rey's flesh is still burning under her hands, so Lauren stops to push herself back to her feet and make a run for it.

"Not this time!" Kensington flips the knife in his hands, throwing it at her.

She moves to deflect it, shifting it mid-throw and sending it off into the storm. Not deterred, Kensington summons a new knife and throws it again. Using the same move, Lauren shouts, "I thought you were done playing games!?"

Kensington smirks. "I am."

A bark causes Lauren to spin around, finding four coyotes at her feet, blood-red eyes staring up at her. She steals a glance at Rey, sliding to place herself in front of him. She goes to conjure something to defend herself, but the games are over, and the coyotes lunge straight for her throat. Ducking, she rushes underneath, tripping on the uneven ground. Once she rights herself, one of the other coyotes snaps at her satchel, biting at the strap and pulling her down. With a death grip on the satchel, she tries to get her feet back under her as it drags her closer to the storm. A sharp pain shoots up her leg as one more coyote grabs her calf, pulling her in the opposite direction for a quick second before she kicks it off. Ignoring the pain of its teeth ripping through her pants, she kicks its face for good measure and rips the strap of the satchel. In the brief moment it takes the coyotes to get their bearings, she takes off towards Hatawa, who's back in his bear form. He charges at the coyotes behind her, knocking them across the ground.

Just behind them, Hongjoong and Minseok continue to fend off another group of coyotes with just their magic and claws. They land a few good bites on them here and there, but they hold their own. Kensington takes matters into his own hands once again and sends another blast of hellfire towards them.

"Hongjoong!" Lauren screams from her spot behind Hatawa.

Hongjoong and Minseok turn to see the fire flying at them while Lauren uses as much of the energy as she has left to push it off course. It doesn't move much, but it's just enough for Minseok to pull Hongjoong aside, tossing him as he then swipes at an approaching coyote. The quick spin leaves him dazed, shaking his head to clear it as he takes stock of their situation. He cannot see the large coyote, further along in its transformation, staking towards him with soft footfalls. Lauren and Minseok spot it, watching as it pushes off the ground and launches for him. Before Lauren can even pull herself to her feet, Minseok runs forward, pushing Hongjoong out of the way with a blast of wind that also sends the coyote skidding through the sand away from them. It stumbles back to an upright position and shakes its head to clear the sand from its blood-red eyes. It looks to Hongjoong, who now lies on the sand closer to Lauren, and then to Minseok and charges. Hongjoong tries to get to his feet while shouting his name in warning. Minseok turns and throws up his arm to block and force it back, but at the last second, the coyote changes its target and sinks its teeth into the exposed skin right below his shoulder.

"No!" Hongjoong continues to try to get his feet under him, but then there's a weight on his back, something holding him down. He barely registers the feeling of heat hovering over him as time slows. The particles of sand and dirt spinning around them appear to hover in place; he watches with wide, scared eyes as the coyote seems to laugh before sinking its teeth down further into the arm. A heart-stopping scream tears from Minseok as blood pours from his arm, soaking into the dirt at his feet as his knees give out with the weight of the coyote on top of him.

Just as quickly as it slowed, time speeds up as rage fills every fiber inside Hongjoong. Channeling all his magic, he shoves the coyote off with a burst of burning black wisps. It howls as it rolls away, shaking to get the black flames off its fur, but Hongjoong pulls himself to his feet and sends another blast of fires at it, sending it yipping off into the storm. With that one dealt with, he spins around and makes for the coyote on Minseok.

Lauren watches, dumbfounded, as Hongjoong charges the large coyote, throwing himself at it with his claws out. Without missing a beat, it tosses Minseok aside and knocks Hongjoong away with a single, heavy paw swipe. Rushing to him, she pulls him back up to his feet. A growl rumbles out of his throat, and the coyote stares him down as it walks towards Minseok. Hongjoong turns into an almost blur as he charges the coyote again, this time landing a good slash across its flank before it knocks him back down. Lauren starts for Minseok only to be stopped by Hatawa's cry of pain; two coyotes hold him down, teeth sinking into his back.

Standing there, Lauren looks around at everyone, frozen and unsure who to help.

It's the end, she thinks, even as the storm is weakening and fading, the sun coming back with glaring brightness; it's over.

"I think you should surrender now," Kensington says, strolling towards Lauren.

She looks around once more and says, "If you want me to surrender, you have to kill me with your own hands."

"That, I can do," he grins.

Lauren takes a deep breath, lifting her head as she lets the satchel fall to her feet. Charging a random spell in her hands, she clenches her fists and waits for him to get close enough to attack. Just as she lifts her hand to fire, something flies by her head and buries itself into Kensington's shoulder.

An arrow that glows with gold dust.

Others follow that single arrow aimed at Kensington and the coyotes. Sun streams into the area with a bright flash as the storm breaks, dust and sand falling straight out of the sky and creating a small cloud of cover for the coyotes to retreat.

"I am not done," Kensington declares, snapping the arrow still in his shoulder. "I will return, and all of you will pay for this! Mark my words! We are not done! We cannot be stopped!" He shifts into a vulture again and takes off towards the sun with a gust of wind, arrows following.

Witches cloaked in sand-white outfits and headwear that obscure their faces sweep through the scene and pick off the coyotes that continue to fight. There's at least a few dozen of them, moving around to cover each member of their coven, checking their vitals, and chasing the straggling coyotes. With the threats neutralized, Hongjoong rushes to Minseok's side, and Nico makes his way to Rey, collapsing next to him.

At that moment, the exhaustion hits Lauren, looking at all the faces of their coven and the damage done. One second, she's looking over the bloody scene, and the next, her knees give out. She falls to the floor as her eyes roll back, body limp as it hits the dirt.

High Coven

"You sent us into a trap!" Hongjoong screams, eyes wild with adrenaline.

The High Priest standing before him, a tall man with dark skin and black hair tied up in a ponytail, looks unimpressed. "We were not aware the coyotes had advanced that far in the transformation process."

"But you knew." He jabs a finger at him. "You knew, and you still sent us in! I swear if any, and I mean ANY of my coven members die, I am going to rain hell fire on you!"

"We have the best healers. No need to worry about your stray witches," the High Priest waves him off, fueling his rage.

"Coven," he corrects through clenched teeth. "My coven. I don't give a damn what your books say anymore. This is my family and my coven."

The High Priest says nothing in response.

Lauren stands behind Hongjoong on shaky legs. The coven Knights refuse to let her or Hongjoong join the rest of their coven. As soon as they were guided through the lone white marble door–that serves as a barrier and portal–the Coven Knights rushed the rest down a hallway on their left. Before they could even move to follow them, the high Priest came down the main hallway and stopped them.

The High Coven's home is disturbingly white and clean. The entryway stretches off towards another set of doors, a light wood tone with streams of sunlight reaching through. More hallways line each side, some with doors and some without. The one the Coven Knights went through is wider than the rest and well lit.

A throat clears from behind the High Priest, and a new witch emerges from one of the many hallways.

"Looks like the council is ready for you."

"Council?" Lauren gives an exasperated sigh. "They want us to present our evidence now? In this state?"

"Yes, the Inquisitors think it would be better to get everything out of the way now." He motions for them to follow as he turns and follows the other witch through an open hallway. "They want to go over everything while it's still fresh in your minds. You two have the most crucial evidence, so your stories are the most important."

Lauren gives a shaky breath and picks up her satchel. As she begins to follow, she stumbles, and Hongjoong is quick to catch her. He keeps a hand on her back as he glares at the High Priest, who doesn't break stride. They follow him through a couple of different doorways before he turns a corner into a dimly lit hall. There's one single light in the entire hallway and two doors on either side of it in the middle. The end of the hall is dark, but there's nothing beyond it other than a wall.

"There's an inquisitor in each room," the High Priest explains. "Each of you pick a room, give your testimonies, and then you can go check on your friends."

"Coven," Hongjoong continues to glare at the High Priest as he turns back and leaves. Once he's out of sight, he helps Lauren walk up to one door and then takes her by the shoulders. "If you finish before me, wait here, okay?"

Lauren nods. He pulls her into a hug. They hold each other for a few moments before separating and entering the rooms.

Both come face to face with identical-looking witches: long white hair, piercing blue eyes, and pale skin, dressed in simple light blue cloaks which shine despite the poor lighting. They sit in front of a desk, devoid of anything but a single notebook. There's a single chair, cushioned unlike that of an interrogation room, but just as intimidating. Hongjoong raises a brow at the inquisitor; she motions him to take a seat. In her room, Lauren hobbles to the lone chair, collapsing with a groan as she reaches down to press on the bandaged bite on her leg. The Inquisitors take them each in, looking over their disheveled, tired state before opening the notebook and taking out a pen.

"Let's start from the beginning."

~

By the time Lauren steps out of the room, it feels like it's been hours, but there's no window to gauge the time of day and no clocks in sight. She takes a second to scan the small hallway, and not seeing

Hongjoong, leans against the wall and lifts her leg to relieve the pressure.

A few minutes later, the other door is thrown open and Hongjoong steps out, shoulders tense as he rolls his neck.

"Done?"

He looks to Lauren, and his shoulders drop. "Done."

"Did they say anything to you about the coven?" She asks.

He shakes his head as he walks up to her. "No, only questions about our old covens and my history. So many questions." He shakes his head and takes her hand. "Let's go find our coven."

They walk back the way they came through the empty white halls. Hongjoong keeps their pace slow for Lauren and checks each hallway for any signs that would lead them to the medical ward. As they turn a corner and finally find themselves back in the entryway, they stop. By the tall marble doors is Hatawa. He turns at the sound of their shoes on the stone and freezes.

None of them move.

Then Hatawa breaks out into a broad smile and rushes to them. They let him crash into them with his arms wide open, wrapping them in a tight hug. Even though he's heavier, both accept the weight and hold on to him; Lauren has a death grip on his tattered jacket as tears begin to form again.

"Are they okay?" Hongjoong asks, voice shaking as he rubs Hatawa's back.

Hatawa squeezes them, sniffles, and shakes his head. "I don't know. They're all in the medical ward still. They're going to set the whole coven up in their own room, but as soon as they treated my wounds, I left to find you guys." He lifts his weight off them and pulls back to see their faces. "I didn't want you two to be alone when you came out."

With a choked sob, Lauren curls closer to them, placing herself between their warmth as she lets herself cry.

Hongjoong tosses his head back as he blinks away his own tears. He takes a second to collect himself before he says, "Okay, let's go to them."

It takes Lauren a minute to get her emotions under control enough to move. She retakes Hongjoong's hand as Hatawa leads the way through the pristine, white halls. Not far down the hall the rest of them went, are two frosted doors that read 'Medical Ward.' As soon as they step through the doors, a young witch sitting at the main desk flashes them a smile.

"Welcome. The council said you should be finished with the Inquisitors." He stands up and grabs a clipboard. "Your injuries are not bad, but the nurses will want to look you over again. Fighting Hell Hounds is quite dangerous." Despite the seriousness of his words, there's still a polite smile plastered on his face. "Follow me."

"I know we need to be checked out," Hongjoong steps forward, "but I need to see my coven first."

The witch's eyes soften. "You will; we'll have the doctor and nurses look you over in your private room. Some of your coven is already there. Please, follow me."

Similar to the rest of what they've seen, the medical ward walls are a sterile white, and just like human hospitals, the lights are set to a sharp brightness. Unlike the rest of the halls however, there are a considerable amount of witches milling around the different rooms and stations. Soon enough, they reach a set of light wood double doors with several panes of glass, through which one of their coven members can be seen standing in the middle of the room where he's silhouetted by lingering rays of sunlight that stream in through a small window on the far end of the room. Hongjoong lets go of Lauren's hand to rush past Hatawa and shove open the doors.

Joshua stands in the middle of the room, one arm wrapped around his waist and the other resting on it as he bites his nails. There's a bandage wrapped around his head, which turns as soon as the door opens. For a second, he looks scared, but upon seeing the three of them, he breaks out into a smile.

"I'm so glad you're okay," Joshua says, opening his arms as Hongjoong steps up to hug him.

Lauren gives him a smile as Hatawa leads her to the first bed on their right. A nurse comes through the door and asks to see her leg. As she lets the witch look her over, she takes stock of who all is in the room: Joshua stands with Hongjoong,

Hatawa is beside her, Azrael lies across the room on the bed in front of her. He gives her a bright smile and wave, which she returns. On the two beds next to him are Rey and Nico, both lying on their sides and facing each other with their hands intertwined in the space between them.

The witch that led them in lifts his clipboard and says, "I'm sure you want to know how everyone is fairing, so I'll start with the rabbit here," he gestures to Azrael. "His leg was crushed. An easy fix; he just needs to keep it in the cast until it heals properly. The golden retriever," he points to Joshua, "has a concussion. We don't believe it's any concern, but he'll need to be watched closely for any signs of head trauma over the next few days."

"Do all healers here call patients by their animal and not their name?" Hongjoong asks.

"It's easier until we have all your names down on record. You can correct it later. Now, moving on," he turns to Rey and Nico, "the huskies sustained serious injuries to their faces."

The pair stir, and it's then Lauren realizes that they're awake. Nico shifts closer to the edge of his bed as Rey squeezes his hand. Neither can see through the bandages. There's a patch of Rey's hair over the burnt side that's turned a stark white, and despite the bandages, there's a deep slash across Nico's cheek that couldn't be bandaged over as his eyes have been.

"They've both lost vision in their affected eyes," the witch continues, "and both the burn and the slashes will scar. Magic can work wonders, but scar tissue is still a bit of a struggle. The surgeons did their best, but even trying to save their vision given the intensity of dark magic used was taxing."

Once the nurse is done with her, Lauren moves to Rey and Nico and crouches between them. She gently takes their hands in hers and squeezes them so they know she's there.

"Which leaves you three," the witch concludes. "All your injuries were not as serious as the rest, hence why the Inquisitors wanted to see you so soon. We will definitely want to monitor the Hell

Hound bites." He draws out the last word as he looks through the papers on the clipboard.

Hatawa lets the nurse look over his wounds once more, while Hongjoong guides Joshua to sit on the bed next to Hatawa's.

One unspoken question hangs in the air.

"I'm a little scared to ask," Hongjoong says, "but what about the other two? Tamryn, the owl, and Minseok, the tiger. Where... where are they?"

"In surgery still," he says. "The tiger should be out soon."

"Can you tell us their condition at least?"

"Until they finish the surgery, we don't want to tell you anything."

Nico shifts his grip in Lauren's hold to squeeze her hand as Rey reaches out, taking a second to find her shoulder before he squeezes it. She moves one of her hands from their grasp to rest on his and gives him a squeeze in return. Hatawa reaches for Hongjoong and rubs his arm as he sits down next to him as the witch leaves them alone with the nurse.

"I guess we just wait," Azrael sighs, sinking into the bed. "I hate this."

Joshua hums in agreement.

The nurse checks on all their vitals, but doesn't make Lauren move from her spot as she sets her up with an IV. Then she leaves as well. As the door closes, the silence bleeds in. There's no noise from the hallway and barely any movement from them. The air grows more tense with each passing minute. There's nothing to talk about, nothing to discuss, only silent prayers that Minseok and Tamryn will be okay.

It isn't a long wait, but it feels like hours. The doors open, and they roll a bed in. Hongjoong jumps to his feet and moves to see which member it is. As quickly as he stood up, his whole body freezes. On the bed is Minseok. The nurses are careful as they move him into the room and situate the bed next to Joshua. His face is pale, sweat beads on his hairline, and his eyes are hazy from the medication being pumped into him. But none of that is why Hongjoong continues to stare with wide eyes: Minseok's left arm is gone.

"We did what we could," a doctor says, "but even with our magic, it was too shredded to reattach or fix his arm. The Hell Hound left little in the area to work with. I'm sorry."

An icy chill sweeps through the room.

Minseok turns his head to Hongjoong, his eyes shine with tears as Hongjoong takes a few cautious steps toward him. Minseok starts crying so Hongjoong rushes the last few steps and falls to his knees. With no hand to grab on this side, his hands hover over where it would be, unsure what to do as Minseok sobs out. "I'm reaching for you, but there's nothing there."

"Shh, shh, it's okay. I'm here." Tears pool in his eyes as he pulls himself up to sit next to Minseok. He takes hold of his right hand, gripping it as he lays his head on his chest. "I'm here. I'm right here."

Fear paralyzes Lauren. Her grip slackens as her brain process Minseok's state. She thinks of how injured Tamryn was, how much worse his state was. If they couldn't save his arm...

"Hey," Nico croaks, tightening his hold on her hand. "Stay with us Lauren, it's okay."

Hatawa walks over to Lauren. He crouches next to her and wipes away her tears. "We don't know anything yet, don't panic. Breath, please," he rubs her back and guides her breathing until she stops shaking.

"Go lay down," Rey says. "You need to rest."

With a meek "okay," she lets Hatawa lift her off the floor and walk her back to the bed. She wipes her face a couple of times, trying not to think the worst, even as Minseok and Hongjoong's sobs fill the room with dread.

Eventually, night falls, and dinner is brought to them as a new nurse looks them all over. Minseok's pain medication puts him to sleep alongside Rey and Nico. Azrael and Joshua both stay in bed and let the nurse check them both for any signs of further head trauma. The food served isn't terrible; it's not a home-cooked meal, but it is enough. Lauren tries her best to eat, even though it makes her nauseous with every bite. Hongjoong gets a chair and sits on

Minseok's right side, holding his hand.
Hatawa monitors everyone for the rest of
the evening as they wait for any news on
Tamryn.

Hours pass.

The night drags on.

The few not on medication stay awake,
waiting.

Then the doors open.

This time, the bed being wheeled in has
more bells and whistles on it: wires hang off
the side, and there's a cart full of monitors
alongside it. They wheel the bed past
Lauren. Her breath catches at the sight of an
oxygen mask and tank. Tamryn's skin is
paler than usual; he looks too stiff, too still.
Once they situate the bed next to Rey's,
Lauren puts her feet on the floor. There's a
lump in her throat as she pushes off the
bed, grabs the IV stand, and shuffles across
the room.

Hongjoong watches her, afraid to move
from Minseok's side but worried for her.

The nurses leave, and the same doctor
as before speaks. "Despite all the odds, he
pulled through."

Joshua glares.

"He did pull through. This is all just," he gestures to everything, "uh, precautionary."

Azrael looks him over and says, "He's in a coma, isn't he?"

"Yes."

By this point, Lauren is next to him. Her hands shake as she touches his face, pushing his hair back as she looks for any signs of consciousness.

"It's a medically induced coma. He should wake up within a day or two. The surgeons had to use both human methods and magic to seal his lungs. The Hell Hound punctured them in quite a few places, but we were able to patch and stitch. The biggest thing is the amount of blood he lost." He sighs. "He will need to be watched carefully to make sure he doesn't open any of his stitches. Patching up lungs isn't something we do often, especially ones done by Hell Hounds, but with the right care, he should make a full recovery in time."

"Are you," Hongjoong stresses the next word, "positive he'll wake up?"

"Yes," he answers. "His body is just in distress, and with the damage to his lungs, he'll need the oxygen mask until he can breathe on his own."

Lauren covers her mouth to hold in a sob.

Hongjoong takes a moment to breathe before saying, "As I told the High Priest that met us at the door, if any of my coven members die, there will be hell to pay." He holds the doctor's gaze for only a moment before growling, "Get out."

Lauren situates herself on the floor next to Tamryn, taking his hand and placing a soft kiss on it before laying her head on the bed. Hongjoong instructs Hatawa to grab her a chair to sleep in and then tells everyone to get some sleep.

"We did our job," Hongjoong says, trying for reassurance. "We're done, and we are all still here. Let's get some rest."

Book of Covens

Even though their sleep is restless, they all eventually succumb to exhaustion. Hongjoong does his rounds to check on everyone after sunrise before the nurses come back, and after breakfast, Rey and Nico both get their heads unwrapped. As soon as they can see each other, they break down. The nurse gives them a minute to sit together before she takes and wraps their heads again, keeping their good eyes uncovered this time. Lauren doesn't leave Tamryn's side, but Rey makes her sit between his and Tamryn's beds so he can comfort her better. Tamryn's vitals don't change. They are stable, but they don't change. When lunch is brought in, everyone besides Tamryn is awake. Minseok struggles. Even though his right arm is his dominant, it keeps throwing him off when he tries to reach for something he would usually grab with his left. Hatawa and Joshua help the others eat and take care of themselves while Hongjoong focuses on Minseok.

The day passes without incident, and as they're eating dinner, Tamara enters.

Hongjoong's reaction is instant; his face drops as he abruptly stands up.

"Let me start." She holds up her hands as the door closes behind her. "I did not know those were Hell Hounds. Turns out, that was on a need-to-know basis, and some of us were not informed. We have been having many conversations about withholding information with everything going on."

Nico sighs. "I don't know if that's supposed to be comforting or not."

Tamara laughs and drops her hands. "A little comforting, I hope. I am on your side, after all. Out of all the witches I have helped throughout the years, I think you might be my favorite group."

"Coven," Azrael corrects, earning a smile from Hongjoong as he sits back down.

"Right, which is why I am here. Hongjoong," she walks to him. "The High Coven is extremely impressed with you and what you have done. They have seen your skills as a leader and know you have been interested in the High Coven since you were young. So they want to offer you a place among our ranks."

Before anyone can even react, Hongjoong declines. "Yeah, no. Had you asked me even a year ago, I might have said yes, but this is my coven. I'm not leaving them."

"Hongjoong," Minseok grips his arm. "You've wanted this since you were a kid, are you sure?"

He looks at Minseok, really looks at him, and smiles. "I'm positive; I have everything I could ever need. A coven of witches that love each other like family and you," he takes Minseok's hand in his, "the love of my life."

Minseok's eyes widen. "Love of your life? Hongjoong, do you- really?"

With a broad smile, Hongjoong nods his head. "I love you, Minseok."

"I love you too," Minseok says, voice breathless as he gives a weak tug on Hongjoong's hands. Getting the signal, Hongjoong leans forward and gives Minseok a soft kiss, doing his best not to agitate any of his injuries. Minseok holds onto his hand like a lifeline.

"Mom and Dad are finally together!" Nico cheers from across the room. Then he turns to Azrael and states, "You owe my fifty bucks," which snaps the tension as the coven bursts into laughter.

"I'm actually glad this is your decision," Tamara says with a smile, "because there is another offer we have for all of you."

"Oh," Azrael sits up straighter, "do tell."

"Well, it wasn't originally on the table, but after they saw you all together and realized how close you are, the High Coven is offering to put your coven in the book. You would become an official coven, and we would even help you find your own land."

Skeptical, as always, Rey asks, "And the catch to this is?"

"There isn't one unless you count being a part of the trial one, but that should have already been a given since you all have so much evidence. What I am surprised about is that all of you come from covens that have larger roles to play in the rebellion. Some we have already captured. Like their coven," she makes a motion towards Rey and Nico, "never had the best defenses, so we already have them in lockdown and his coven," this time, she points to Joshua, "was actually quite easy to get to flip on some others."

"But for the rest of us, we'll have to testify and give evidence," Azrael says as he crosses his arms.

Tamara nods. "You stay for the trial, and we can put you in the books and set you up with a home as soon as the main trials are finished. I think it's quite fair, actually."

Hongjoong sits back. "I almost feel like this is the High Coven's way of keeping an eye on us. Not every group of witches can fight off Hell Hounds and survive, so I'm sure they'd rather be our friends than our enemies."

"Which is fair," Lauren adds.

Hatawa clears his throat. "I think we should do it. That way, we aren't constantly fighting to prove we're a coven. We can go about our lives without having to be called strays anymore. It's a once-in-a-lifetime opportunity."

"He's right," Minseok turns to Hongjoong. "We do this, and we won't be bothered again."

Hongjoong takes a breath as he looks at each member of his coven. He takes a minute to gauge all their facial expressions before turning to Tamara. "Alright. We'll take part in the trials, but I want the coven ceremony first."

Tamara's face brightens. "Perfect! I will let them know, and we will get the ceremony set up within a few days." She sweeps out of the room in a sudden motion with a bright smile still on her face.

"Is it weird that she's so happy about this?" Joshua asks.

"Maybe," Rey shrugs, "but we're gonna be an official coven, so I honestly don't care." Then, with a broad smile, he sinks back into his bed as Nico laughs.

Lauren looks down at Tamryn. She tries not to think of what it would be like to have the coven without him, but he has shown no signs of waking up, and the fear is eating her alive.

Nothing changes overnight.

By the next afternoon, Azrael is allowed to walk, and Joshua is given the all-clear. A council member comes in to take down all their information for the coven book: age, date of birth, original coven, specialties, and such. Joshua answers most of the questions for Tamryn's portion with help from the others, and Lauren just stays by his side, unwilling to move.

Night falls once more.

The final nurse of the night informs Hongjoong that Nico and Rey should both be rid of their bandages by the end of the next day and plan to hold their coven ceremony as soon as Tamryn is awake. He thanks her before settling in as she dims the lights and leaves.

The night wears on, and soon Lauren is the only one still awake. She sits in the chair beside Tamryn, legs curled underneath herself as she watches him. There's a large part of her rational brain that knows he'll wake up, but the smaller portion, the fear that he just won't, is winning out with each passing hour. His skin color has improved, she tries to remind herself, meaning the fluids are getting to him despite his state.

With a sigh, she retakes his hand.

"Tamryn," she whispers. "I don't know if you can hear me. I read somewhere once that there's a chance you can, so I just... I want to tell you we all miss you. I know your body is healing, but we really need you to come back." She takes a breath and wipes away her tears. "I really need you to come back. I don't know if I can handle losing you before we even got a chance.

"On top of everything else these last few months have put me through, I cannot lose you." His fingers twitch in her grasp, but it isn't the first time his unconscious body has responded. She reaches up to brush his hair back, and his face scrunches up. Her hand stops moving, leaving his hair to fall back as his face relaxes, but then it scrunches again, and his fingers twitch.

"Tamryn?"

His face twists again. Then his mouth opens, and he takes in a shallow breath.

"Tamryn?" she asks again, voice wavering as she slides her feet out from under herself and leans closer to him.

It takes his eyes a few seconds, but they flutter open. His vision is hazy to start; it takes a few blinks for him to register where he is, but once he does, his eyes find Lauren's face, and he smiles.

"Hey." His voice is dry, fogging up the mask.

Tears fall from her eyes as her whole body relaxes. "Hey yourself. You had us really worried. I'm so happy to see you awake."

"How long was I out?"

"A few days." She brushes his hair back as he groans in pain. "Your lungs took quite a beating, so don't breathe too deep."

He nods and closes his eyes again as he tries to keep his breathing steady. Trying her best to keep her crying silent and not wake the others, she bites her tongue and wipes away her tears as fast as possible. Tamryn feels her movement and opens his eyes, heart breaking as he watches her. As carefully as he can, he lifts his other hand and reaches over to hold her cheek and wipe away what he can.

"It's okay," he croaks out, coughing at the end with a heavy, shuddering breath.

Fear takes over. She shushes him with a soft voice, "Don't strain yourself. I'm just really happy you're okay." They smile. "You should rest. I need to get a nurse or someone. I'm the only one up, so just," she looks around to double-check and squeezes his hand as she turns back. "Let me get someone to check on you, and then we can rest, okay?" He nods his head, letting his hand fall back to his side with a careful breath.

Every fiber of her being tells her to not let go, but she fights her fear and places a kiss on his head before swiftly and silently exiting the room. As she locates the nurse and lets her know Tamryn is awake, she also warns her that everyone is sleeping. They make sure their steps are quiet as they reenter the room and go over to him. Tamryn lets the nurse check him over and listens as she explains what they've done to keep his lungs working, and as soon as she's done, he turns his focus back to Lauren.

"This may sound morbid, but I'm really glad the last thing I saw before everything went black was you," he says, voice low and words coming out slowly. "If that had been the end, then at least you would be my final thoughts."

"Come on," Lauren wipes away fresh tears, "I'm really tired of crying, and you aren't getting rid of me that easily."

He smiles under his mask, "I'm glad."

"Get some sleep." She scoots the chair closer, not letting go of his hand. "I'll fill you in on everything when you wake up. I'll be by your side all night, I promise."

He hums in contentment and lets the medication take over as it puts him to sleep. It isn't long after that she joins him, head resting on his shoulder.

In the morning, when Tamryn opens his eyes, everyone is ecstatic. More tears flow as they all hug him and praise the higher deities for their luck. They fill him in on everyone else's injuries and the deal they cut with the High Coven. In true Tamryn fashion, he tries to keep the mood light by drilling Joshua on his answers to make sure he knows them, while Nico boasts about correcting him on a few. Warmth fills the room, a warmth that none of their injuries can hinder. Rey and Nico both get their bandages removed, revealing their new battle scars - which Azrael happily points out are a matching set.

As the sun begins its descent, everyone is escorted out of the Medical Ward. Tamryn is in a wheelchair with his oxygen mask - a precaution - and Azrael on crutches. They're led back into the white halls of the coven home and then down the long entryway towards the light, wooden doors at the end. The nurses accompanying them open the doors, and they're all hit with an intense burst of sunlight.

The main building wraps around a large flourishing courtyard with stone buildings, homes, lush grassy areas, and trees in full bloom, despite it being the middle of winter. The sun soaks into their cool skin as they walk through the town towards the center, where an elevated wooden platform stands. On the platform is a stone lectern that holds a large white book that Tamara is looking through.

"It's time," she says as she closes the book and looks at them. "This will be a simplified ceremony, but I need to recite all the proper scripting to make it official. Normally we would have an audience." She looks over the mostly empty area. There are witches around, but they're all going about their daily routines. "But, seeing as this is rather abrupt, we don't have too much time before the trial starts."

They all give their words of understanding as they make their way up onto the platform with her. It takes Azrael and Tamryn a minute to follow the rest, but they all form into a semi-circle once they do. Hongjoong stands in the middle, directly in front of the lectern and Tamara.

"Ready when you are," he says.

Tamara smiles and opens the book to the first page. "A coven is a group of souls that were once family in a life long since passed. To create a coven is to find your true family among all the witches of the world. The blood of the coven will always be thicker than the water of the womb. Today we induct a new coven to the books, another family that has found themselves. Even if your coven never grows beyond those in it today, they are your family from this moment onward." She takes the red tassel hanging from the middle of the book and pulls it to open to a new registry page. "By signing your names here, you agree to release your affiliation with your birth coven and give your all to the coven you have chosen here today. Do you wish to continue?" She takes a quill out from under the lectern and holds it out.

Hongjoong doesn't hesitate. He takes the quill as Tamara spins the book to face them. He signs and then helps Minseok sign his name. Next, he passes the quill to Joshua, then to Azrael, then Rey and Nico, who have to help each other with their lack of vision. Hatawa takes it next, and then he carries the book to Tamryn for him and Lauren to sign. Tamryn thanks him and gives him a smile under his oxygen mask. Tamara takes the quill and book from Hatawa and signs it herself before closing it, which releases a shower of white sparks as it seals itself.

"Welcome to the book of covens."

Epilogue

The sun hides behind a layer of dark gray clouds, which blanket the mountain tops of San Bernardino's National Forest. Snowflakes fall in graceful swirls all around the town of Big Bear and its lake. They rest on the frozen surface, treetops, and add to the thick layer of crystal snow already covering the ground. Despite the cloud cover and late hour, there's enough light to see through the forest to a lone log cabin high up on the mountain side, far away from the bustle of the main city and its holiday travelers. It's surrounded by a dense expanse of trees, but in the backyard, a small stone staircase leads up to an overlook. From there, the lake is clearly visible in all it's sparkling glory.

On this overlook, stands Lauren, but she isn't looking at the view. At her feet is a small slab of concrete, carved with the names 'Annabelle Muldoon' and 'Suho Kim.' The carvings are done by two different hands, each parent's name written by the child they raised, and at the bottom is a collection of wildflowers wrapped in white cloth.

Lauren stares down at it with one arm wrapped around her waist and her other hand is busy twisting the pendant of her necklace. She's silent; lost in her thoughts of all that's transpired in the past two months.

"You're going to catch a cold," Tamryn says from behind her as a heavy coat is draped over her shoulders.

She doesn't jump, but she dose turn her head and smile. "It's not that cold," she says as he leans down to place a gentle kiss on her cheek. The warmth of his lips on her cold skin brings her back to reality and she quickly turns to face him, holding onto the coat so it doesn't fall. "Wait, yes, it is. You shouldn't be out here!"

Tamryn huffs and rolls his eyes. "My lungs can handle a little bit of cold air."

"I'd rather not push it," she retorts, taking his hand to pull him back towards the staircase. "Until the High Coven doctor gives you a clean bill of health, I'm not taking any chances. Why did you come out here anyway?"

"Oh right." He lets her guide them down the icy stairs as he explains, "Minseok is currently trying to do the cooking on his own."

Lauren pauses on the last step and tosses her head back, grumbling, "Stubborn healer."

With a laugh, he tugs her hand as he makes for the back door. "Hongjoong is resting and Minseok doesn't want to disturb him, so I thought it'd be best to bring you in."

"Thank you," she turns his head as he pulls open the sliding glass door and gives him a kiss.

"Get a room!"

Pulling back, she finds Nico and Rey on the same couch she left them, with cheeky grins as they watch her and Tamryn. They're situated in the middle of the long couch and they placed themselves so that each of their blind eyes are next to each other, a new habit they came up with to make sure no one sneaks up on them. Lauren tries not to think about it as she steps inside and shakes her head.

"Like you two have any room to talk," she calls as she slips off both Tamryn's coat and her thinner one she had on. Then she turns to Tamryn who's untying his boots, "And you, go sit and drink the tea Minseok brewed. Dinner should be ready fairly soon."

"Yes ma'am." He gives a smile and small salute as he pulls off his boots and places them on the rack Minseok created for their enormous collection of shoes.

As he walks forward into the large and open living room, she turns right and walks into the kitchen. It's separated from the living room by a solid wall, but both sides are open to the back door entry and a spacious dining area. The kitchen itself is up to date for a log cabin, with black modern appliances and black granite counters which accent the light oak cabinetry. Minseok stands in front of the stove, where a large stew is boiling, and is clearly struggling with cutting the carrots.

She announces her presence by saying, "I assume you cut everything else on your own?"

Minseok jumps, dropping the knife on the counter before he turns to her. "Uh, maybe? But it wasn't too bad. I can do it."

"I know you can," she walks up and takes the knife, "but you don't have to. We discussed this," she begins to cut the carrots as Minseok watches her, "I am here to help with all the things you do for the coven. We're a pair now."

That makes Minseok smile, but as quickly as it grew it drops as what's left of his left arm twitches. It didn't take them long to learn that when the nub of his arm twitches, it means his brain sent a signal to move it and it almost always causes him to fall into a bad headspace.

Lauren sets the knife down instantly. "Do you want Hongjoong?"

A few tears begin to pool in his eyes, but he blinks them away and shakes his head. "No, I'll be fine. That meeting this morning took a lot out of him, he needs to rest."

Footsteps approach them from the dinging area followed by Hongjoong's groggy voice. "Too late, I'm already up," he says as he walks up to Minseok and wraps his arms around his waist, resting his head on his chest.

"Babe," Minseok sighs, "you need to rest."

"I did," Hongjoong mumbles into Minseok's shirt, "and now I want to hold you, sue me."

Their soft laughter fills the kitchen with warmth as Minseok shakes his head. Lauren instructs them to go sit in the living room and send Hatawa over to help her finish cooking. He comes in a few minutes later with confused look on his face.

"Hatawa," Lauren draws his name out as she narrows her eyes at him. "Are you still thinking about it?"

"Of course I am! It's super confusing," he grumbles. "I swore there was a coven on this land and I know the High Coven said it wasn't in the books, but I just..." he trails off and runs a hand through his hair.

"Stir," she points to the stew and holds out a ladle, which he takes as he joins her at the stove. "Look, I wish I could calm your brain and say it's just something you misremembered, but I know it's not."

"Exactly! And my mom–"

"If you call your mother again to ask her, I am going to take away your phone privileges," she threatens with a sharp look that makes Hatawa look down at stew.

"I just," he pauses, demeanor growing solemn. "I just don't want the High Coven to have set us up or put us in danger. We've been through so much. I want us to be safe."

Lauren's heart swells and drops at the same time. "We'll be okay, and if something happens, well, at least we know a little bit more about what's really out there," she pauses to put the carrots and final touches into the stew. "And I think we did pretty good for being unprepared, so next time we'll be ready, and I can protect you like you did me."

"Gods no," Hatawa gives a wet laugh, wiping away his growing tears. "None of us need to go to that length again. I think we've all had enough near death experiences for the next hundred years."

She does her best to keep the conversation flowing after that, never letting the smile fall from his face. They finish the stew and biscuits, set up the dining room for all nine of them, and then call everyone to eat.

Once everyone gets situated around the table, squeezing into the small available space as best they can – Azrael plans to make a bigger custom table that fits them all and more, in case the coven grows – Hongjoong stands up to address everyone.

"I have to say," he starts, "joining the book and gaining our own land wasn't a goal I had in mind, but it's nice to be recognized. We are a coven and family, and no signature is going to take that away from us. We've been through a lot, but I'm happy we're still here, together."

"Here, here!" Joshua cheers.

"And I know we missed Christmas," Hongjoong continues, "but it is New Year's Eve and I think this year is going to be a nice fresh start for us."

"Unless some ancient native coven is living here and we don't know," Hatawa mutters under his breath, to which Hongjoong rolls his eyes.

"Yes, paranoid one, unless some ancient coven comes for us," Hongjoong resists the urge to sigh and says, "other than that, it's a new year, new start, and hopefully some peaceful time to relax."

Nico asks, "While I love your speech, can we eat now? I'm starving."

"You're always starving," Minseok says as Hongjoong sits back down. "You are going to eat us out of all our savings at some point."

"Hopefully not," Hongjoong looks scared at the thought, but smiles none the less. "Yes, I'm done. Dig in, it's our first real meal since moving in so let's enjoy it."

Without any hesitancy, the huskies dig in first.

They all start eating, passing the biscuits around and helping each other fill their bowls. Similar to their last holiday together, the laughter and conversation flows with ease and the addition of a ninth voice doesn't offset any of the balance they had. Tamryn keeps a hand on Lauren's knee through the dinner, a tether for them both to hold onto. Minseok and Hongjoong sit noticeably closer than they had before, just like Nico and Rey always have. The differences in the coven would stand out to anyone who had seen them before they met

Epilogue

Lauren, but it's all minor changes in their minds.

They've never been closer, everything feels like it's finally fallen into place, and nothing can come between them now.

ABOUT THE AUTHOR

JP Steward is a fresh author with a unique
vision. She's been writing for well over ten years
but has finally begun to branch out into full
published works. Coming from a family of avid
readers, she's spent all her life listening to
people talk shop about books and what they
really wish authors would do. This has helped
her shape her ideas into stories and worlds that
not only she loves, but her readers do too.